USA TODAY BESTSELLING AUTHOR

NANCY WARREN

WHISK
AND REWARD

THE GREAT WITCHES BAKING SHOW
BOOK 9

Whisk and Reward, The Great Witches Baking Show, book 9

ISBN: ebook 978-1-990210-29-7

ISBN: print 978-1-990210-32-7

Cover Design by Lou Harper of Cover Affairs

Ambleside Publishing

INTRODUCTION

Murder, deceit and baking...

It's the big finale of the Great British Baking Contest. Who will win? Who will fall flatter than an eggless soufflé? And will amateur baker and witch Poppy survive to find out?

Dark forces are at work in the picture-perfect village of Broomewode in Somerset. Poppy's in danger, but why? She's getting closer to solving the mystery of her beginnings but so many questions remain. Will she finally meet her birth mother? Who was her father? Is the local coven helping or hindering her search? Will she and sexy Viscount Benedict finally have their first date?

There are old and new mysteries to solve in this final installment of the Great Witches Baking Show.

If you haven't met Rafe Crosyer yet, he's the gorgeous, sexy vampire in *The Vampire Knitting Club* series. You can get his origin story free when you join Nancy's no-spam newsletter at NancyWarrenAuthor.com.

Come join Nancy in her private Facebook group where we talk about books, knitting, pets and life. www.facebook.com/groups/NancyWarrenKnitwits

WHISK AND REWARD

CHAPTER 1

A light drizzle descended on Broomewode Village on Thursday evening, and by the following morning, the rain had gathered speed and volume and the wind blew great billowing sheets of cool water across the sky. Birds tumbled around clouds, and trees shook their leafy tops. "Thoroughly miserable," I complained to Gateau as we drove along the familiar winding lanes that connected Norton St. Philip to Broomewode. She mewled in reply, shifting in the passenger seat to curl into a tighter ball.

My sweet familiar loathed the rain as much as I did. We made a sorry pair. Both of us had been up all night as the summer storm reached a crescendo. She'd scampered around the entire cottage, annoying Mildred, my kitchen ghost, and keeping me awake. Not that I would have had much luck sleeping anyway. This morning was the Earl of Frome's funeral, and I'd been trying to piece together the strange circumstances of his death. I couldn't believe that Katie Donegal, faithful servant to the earl's family for decades, was a murderer, despite the evidence local police detectives had collected.

Katie had been arrested and charged with the earl's murder, causing more shock in Broomewode. I was worried, too, about the earl's son, Benedict. So many responsibilities had been placed on his shoulders overnight, and he was going to have to stay strong today and put on a brave face as his father was laid to rest in front of the village. My heart ached for him.

Actually, my heart just ached. After a rocky start, Benedict had become special to me. And I to him. I still tingled all over when I recalled the passionate kiss we'd shared. Our kiss had changed everything. I was all topsy-turvy, as Mildred had so helpfully pointed out. Dreaming over the stove, dropping my baking utensils. I didn't seem to know my left from my right anymore. If this was what romance did to a girl, well, I could live without the side effects.

It was a difficult time for a budding romance, though. Benedict had been busy with funeral preparations and comforting his mother. For my part, I'd been kept more than busy with extra shifts at the inn. Pavel, the sous-chef, had caught a horrible stomach bug and taken two days off work to recover. Ruta, the head chef, needed all hands on deck to keep the pub's restaurant afloat. Luckily, we weren't fully booked, but it was enough to exhaust a girl.

Now that Pavel was fully recovered, Ruta had given me the day off to go to the funeral and support Benedict. I hadn't breathed a word of our kiss to anyone but Gateau and Mildred (both great secret-keepers, for obvious reasons), but Ruta seemed to sense how important it was for me to be there.

I knew there was going to be a big turnout. Not because the earl was a popular man (he rubbed far too many people the wrong way) but because he was the Earl of Frome. Besides, curiosity would get the better of many people. Broomewode was a small, close-knit community, and his death was a momentous rupture to the way things were run around here. The earl was landlord to many people, an integral part of the traditions that bound the villagers together. Whether you liked the guy or not, you couldn't get away from the earl's impact on daily village life. It was strange to think that big personality was gone.

As I turned into Church Lane, the rain showed no signs of letting up. It wasn't cold, just miserable, and I longed for the sun to make an appearance and brighten this solemn day.

The number of cars on the road doubled the closer I got to the church, and I soon found myself crawling along at a snail's pace, desperately trying to find a good place to park. No doubt a lot of Robert Champney's posh friends had driven here for the occasion. No doubt most of those he'd invited to his final, ill-fated hunt last weekend would be here to pay their final respects.

Gateau roused herself, done with napping, and watched the rain as it tapped against the window. As I found a space my little Renault Clio could just squeeze into, nerves kicked in. My body felt alien to me. I wondered if this was another example of witchiness that I'd never paid attention to before. I was beginning to believe I picked up on people's emotions and on atmosphere more than most. Or maybe it was just a sad day. I'd dressed for mourning. I never usually wore black, certainly not from head to toe, and the simple shift dress my best friend Gina had lent me for the occasion didn't quite suit my shape. It was too long in the waist, too tight on the shoulders. I undid my seat belt and took a quick glance in the overhead mirror. A minimal makeup job had seemed the most modest approach to the day, and I'd blow-dried my brown hair straight so it hung past my shoulders. Maybe that was a mistake. Even a few curls would have felt less solemn.

Gateau meowed loudly.

"Come on, then," I said. "Let's do this."

Okay, it was unorthodox to bring my cat to a funeral. I knew it, but she was more than a pet. Gateau was my familiar, and she helped protect me from harm. She was also very smart and wouldn't annoy anyone. In fact, I doubted the mourners would notice she was there.

I leaned across the seat and opened the passenger door so that she could jump out and switched my sneakers for plain black pumps. Thankful I'd remembered to grab an umbrella, I made my way to the church. Gateau darted out and headed straight for my ankles, circling to avoid the rain. "You're going to have to keep in step with me," I said, "if you want to stay dry." Gateau shot me a withering look, and I bent to pick her up. She settled in my arms, and I stroked her soft fur.

Gateau didn't appreciate being dragged away from our cozy cottage, but I needed some moral support this morning, not to mention some extra protection. I was wearing my amulet and amethyst necklace, of course. But after last week's tractor crash, Joanna's haunting warning to leave Broomewode immediately, followed by her sudden disappearance, I wasn't taking any chances. I felt like someone, or something, was after me. I had to stay alert at all costs. Not that I could trust Joanna, the woman who'd supposedly known my birth mother and who'd met with me last week for coffee. We'd both nearly been killed when a runaway tractor crashed into the tea shop. In fact, Joanna had saved my life. But then she'd mysteriously disappeared. I still hadn't gotten to the bottom of where she was or even who she was. The phone number I had for her was disconnected. No one had seen her. She might have saved my life, for which I owed her big time, but she wasn't trustworthy; that much was for sure.

In the drizzle, the impressive Broomewode Church made a somewhat sinister silhouette on the horizon. It stood on a small rise above the village and was surrounded by an ancient stone border and a steep set of steps, over the top of which an arch of white roses shuddered in the wind. A blue hydrangea bush collected droplets of water. A small graveyard surrounded the left side of the church, its old headstones crumbling and sinking at angles into the earth. The earl would be laid to rest in the family mausoleum. No one but family would be allowed inside.

I joined the throng of people heading to the service. It was a somber sight, all these figures in black sheltering beneath umbrellas. Despite the weather, everyone looked extremely stylish. Dark suits in inky tones, crisp white shirts, black crepe skirts and blouses, sleek minimal dresses. A lot of jewelry was on show: gold glinting at ears, neck, and wrists, flashes of diamonds and deep red rubies. The men wore their hair in smart crops close to the skull, neatly parted and styled. The women's either fell in long sheets like molten gold or steel down their backs or in carefully groomed chignons and sleek bobs. There was a lot of money here, that was for sure. The earl had friends in high places, and London's elite crowd had made the long journey to pay their respects.

Interspersed with the posh set were the locals. Maybe

they weren't so fancily turned out, but people wore their best dark clothes. I recognized the butcher who'd had a running feud with Katie. There was Eve, who normally tended bar at the inn, with Susan Bentley, the farmer. My sister witches both looked sad. Gateau spotted a cozy enclave by the church steps and wriggled in my arms until I set her down. She promptly dashed off to keep dry. At least she'd be nearby during the service.

I felt a rush of relief when I spotted Jonathon Pine and Elspeth Peach beneath the canopy of an enormous branded *The Great British Baking Contest* umbrella. They weren't speaking, and both looked lost in contemplation. I made my way towards them.

Elspeth caught my eye and smiled sadly. "Poppy, dearest," she said softly and opened her arms to embrace me. I felt the slight electric charge I often felt when Elspeth touched me. She and Jonathon were witches (though, obviously, few people knew that) as well as mentors. She kissed both cheeks, and I inhaled her powdery rose scent. Elspeth looked wonderful as usual, in a simple black trouser suit with a string of pearls at her neck, her white hair twisted into an elegant knot at the nape of her neck.

Jonathon grasped my hands. He looked more formal than I'd ever seen him—his trademark indigo jeans replaced by a charcoal suit and black shirt. He pulled back and looked at me quizzically. "I'm just glad we're not here for your funeral. When Katie sent that tractor crashing into the tea shop, she couldn't have known you were inside."

"If it was Katie," I said. "She still maintains her innocence, and it will be months before she's tried."

"The evidence is compelling," he reminded me. "The earl

was planning to fire her. May already have done so, for all we know. After thirty years of service to the family. She lost her mind. Possibly temporarily, but she sent that tractor crashing into the tea shop only because Robert Champney owned it. And then, when the earl was in his glory at his own hunt, she stretched a length of kitchen twine across his path and knocked him from his horse. She may not have intended to kill him, but he hit his head on a stone, poor sod."

From nowhere, the sound of bagpipes echoed through the air. I turned and saw a lone bagpipe player standing near the mausoleum playing "Abide With Me," full of melancholy. We stopped chatting and headed for the church door.

The Countess of Frome, or I supposed vaguely she'd be the Dowager Countess now the earl was dead, and Benedict stood solemnly with the vicar near the entrance to the church. The doors were open wide, and I could see all the way to the front, where a gleaming wooden coffin contained the remains of the earl. Huge pillar candles on either side of the casket added solemnity.

Benedict looked pale in his black suit. He probably hadn't slept properly all week. I longed to comfort him.

We were at the doorway, about to enter the church, when the moment was interrupted by the arrival of a stretch limousine.

"Goodness," Elspeth murmured, "someone decided to arrive in style." She was as much of a celebrity as anyone in England, and she'd arrived discreetly, which showed a lot more class than whoever was making their entrance.

The crowd of us ready to move inside visibly craned forward, all trying to catch a glimpse of whichever celebrity was about to step out from the limo's tinted windows.

The limo driver stepped out and rushed round to open the door, a black umbrella at the ready. One long leg emerged, sheathed in a seamed stocking and crowned by a shiny black stiletto.

There was an audible intake of breath. Who did this lovely leg belong to? An LA film star? A European princess? Could it be a member of the royal family?

The rest of the woman elegantly emerged, and when she stood to full height, I couldn't believe who I was looking at. Dressed like the love child of Sophia Loren and Jackie Kennedy, the woman was wearing huge dark glasses, an achingly chic black dress and a chiffon scarf tied with a flourish over a head of tumbling chestnut curls. Even with the dark glasses and scarf, I'd recognize that head of hair anywhere.

"I don't believe it," I said. "It's Florence."

Elspeth turned to me, eyes twinkling. "My goodness, what an entrance."

"Quite," agreed Jonathon. "But what's with all the pomp and circumstance? She looks more like the earl's widow than his widow does."

Florence stepped to one side, and a man exited the car. In a suit that would have looked at home in a James Bond film, the man was extraordinarily handsome. With silver-streaked black hair and a salt-and-pepper beard, he was at least a decade older than Florence. He clasped her hand and with the other slipped the umbrella from the driver's gloved hand and held it over them both.

"Is that her agent?" Jonathon whispered.

"Looks more like a film producer," Elspeth said. "Surely it's not a new beau. Where does she find the time?"

Florence and her mystery man wasted no time pushing through the mourners, approaching Lady Frome. The bagpipes were still full force, and I held my breath as Florence greeted Evelyn Champney as though they were old friends, pulling the older woman to her bosom. What was Florence thinking? Surely the countess would recoil from this embrace. She'd never even shaken my hand and made it abundantly clear that I wasn't good enough for her son. How could an Italian baking contestant be any more acceptable to her than an American one?

I leaned forward, wishing I could hear their exchange over the sound of the bagpipes. I waited for the inevitable moment that Lady Frome brushed Florence away as if she were a speck of dust on her immaculate dress, but to my amazement, the recent widow leaned against Florence and placed her head on her shoulder—just like I'd seen her do with Katie Donegal. Yet Katie wasn't here. She was locked away, arrested for the earl's murder. I felt my mouth drop open. Lady Frome had only ever treated me with disdain. Yet she was warm and, dare I think it, vulnerable with Florence. How did those two even know each other?

The mystery man shook hands with Benedict. What on earth was going on?

From her dry perch, Gateau watched the scene with the same rapt attention as everyone else gathered outside the church.

I felt a tap on my shoulder and turned to see Hamish, looking very handsome in a dark blue suit. We hugged, and the moment he pulled away, Hamish said, "What on earth is Florence doing with the countess? And why is that man butchering my homeland's beautiful bagpipes?"

I laughed. "Two very good questions. Neither of which I know the answer to."

Hamish shook hands with Jonathon and Elspeth. He looked a little nervous, and then I remembered why. Funeral or no funeral, it was the final weekend of the baking contest. He'd face the stern but fair judgment of my coven sister and brother tomorrow. The contest was down to Hamish and Florence. I didn't want to pick favorites, as I'd grown fond of both of them, but Florence was already acting as though she'd been crowned the winner, and that alone made me hope Hamish had brought his A-game this week.

The bagpipes echoed to an end, and the crowd that had gathered outside the church began to swell and press. The village locals maneuvered themselves to the front, defending their right of place against the Londoners. I realized nearly everyone from Broomewode was at the service.

"All the local businesses are shut," Elspeth said in my ear, reading my mind, as was her way. "Walking through the village this morning was positively spooky. It was like a ghost town."

I looked around us and clocked each familiar face. There was Bernadette from the Broomewode Hall kitchen; Edward the gamekeeper and his girlfriend, Lauren, holding his hand. I wondered whether Broomewode Church would soon have a happier occasion to celebrate. I'd been coming here long enough that I recognized shopkeepers and residents. And then I caught sight of DI Hembly and Sergeant Lane. They looked alert, eyes darting across the crowd.

"Why are the detectives here?" I asked Hamish. "Surely it's not standard practice to attend the funerals of their murder investigations, is it?"

Hamish shook his head. "If that were true, they'd never get any work done with things the way they are around here. No, I reckon they might look like they're just paying their respects, but they're on the lookout for more clues about how the earl died."

"But Katie's in jail."

I felt a firm hand on my shoulder, warm. "Actually, she's out on bail, luvvie."

"Eve," I said, hugging her to me, feeling a rush of affection. I drew back and studied her face. Eve's gray eyes were usually glinting and mischievous, but today they were still and somber. Her preferred long braid hung down over a simple dark smock dress with a silver locket.

"Really?"

Eve nodded. "Benedict got her the best lawyer. I'm not sure whether he believes she killed the earl, but he wanted her to have proper legal representation." Her mouth thinned, and she leaned closer. "He's been a better friend to her than the countess. She's staying at my place, as the countess won't have her back at the hall, of course. Katie wanted to pay her respects today, but I told her to stay away." She lowered her voice and leaned even closer. "She didn't kill Robert Champney. I know it in my bones."

My bones weren't as certain, but they were willing to entertain some doubt. "Then who did?" I asked in case Eve's bones were detectives as well as judges, but she only shook her head.

"That farmer's not here, is he? To pay his respects. The one that caused all the fuss. It was his tractor nearly killed you."

"I believe the police investigated him pretty thoroughly."

She didn't look convinced. "Ask me, they concluded their investigation very quickly. No doubt there was pressure from above." She looked at the sky, but I didn't think she was referring to God. No doubt she meant the Champneys had friends high up in the judicial system. A quick arrest would appease the family.

We both turned to look at the countess, who was still leaning against Florence. Benedict had moved away from his mother and was greeting some of the crowd. He thanked them for coming, told everyone that his father would have been happy to see so many local faces. Shaking hands, exchanging somber nods, he seemed to understand what the people needed from him.

Susan Bentley and her close friend Reginald, a retiree to Broomewode who'd taken up ironwork as a hobby, spoke to Benedict. "Lord Frome," I overheard Reginald say, "we're so sorry for your loss. Robert Champney will be missed by all of us."

"Thank you, Reginald, but please, I'm just Ben. Lord Frome was my father." He placed a hand on Reg's shoulder and then looked around at the crowd, as if in disbelief this many people had turned out for the funeral. He caught my eye and smiled, excusing himself from Susan and Reg.

Elspeth, Jonathon, and Eve appeared to simply melt away, and then it was just Benedict and me, wondering how to greet each other in a crowd. The last time I'd seen him, we'd kissed. I was still dazed by that fact and felt a schoolgirl blush coming on. Major cringe.

Luckily, Benedict was more composed. He took my hands and kissed each cheek. The perfect blend of formal and intimate. He obviously had more clue than I did how we should behave in public. "It's so good to see you," he murmured. "This week has been a challenge. In so many ways."

I told him I could only imagine. We'd exchanged a few texts, but Benedict hadn't talked much about his feelings. I guessed he'd been raised to maintain a stiff upper lip. But in person, he was more relaxed.

"I still can't quite believe it," he said quietly. "My father was so robust and in the best of health. Then...well, you know."

I took his hand again and squeezed it. "I am truly sorry for your loss. But you are going to be fine," I said.

Benedict smiled, but it quickly faded. I followed the direction of his hard gaze. Florence and her mystery man had finally left the countess's side, probably because she'd turned her attention to a distinguished-looking older man. He looked grave and well-groomed in an expensive suit. There was something vaguely familiar about him. Or was it that everyone looked the same in dark suits?

"Who's that?" I asked.

Benedict raised one brow ever so slightly. "My parents' financial advisor, Harrison Zucker."

The name Harrison rang a bell. And then I remembered —he was one of the gentlemen at the earl's breakfast after the hunt only a week ago. Now it seemed an eternity had passed since I'd watched the horses, riders, and hunt followers set out for a day of recreation. I'd been reassured no fox would be harmed or killed. Little had I known it was the earl I should have worried about.

"He looks to be more of an old family friend?"

"An old goat would be more accurate. He's been hanging

around Mother like a fly around an open jar of honey. Father's not even in his grave yet."

I had a low opinion of the countess, but surely not even she would stoop so low as to flirt at her husband's funeral? "Maybe he's helping her with her finances, now she's a widow," I said, trying to be diplomatic. There'd be death duties, I imagined, though I didn't know much about English law. Benedict just shook his head, not taking his eyes away from the couple. I had to admit it didn't look like the new widow and her financial advisor were talking about money, somehow.

"He asked her to marry him years ago, but she chose my father."

Hmm. That explained the odd chemistry. Now she was free to marry again. It didn't look like Harrison Zucker was planning to wait to renew his addresses.

Benedict glanced around. "I'm surprised Charles Radlier isn't challenging him to a duel. He's been hanging around Mother too." He looked disgusted. "Father's only been dead a week."

"Is he an old suitor too?" Charles was the Master of the Hunt. I hadn't noticed him hanging around Lady Frome last week, though the day had been derailed.

I could imagine Evelyn Champney receiving male attention. She was an attractive woman, if you liked the cold, snobby type. She must have been a knockout in her day.

"I believe he's more interested in Mother's money. I hear Charles is broke. There's no love lost between Charles and Harrison."

"Love and money," I said, "two powerful forces." And I knew a thing or two about powerful forces myself.

Benedict cleared his throat. "Poppy, I was hoping that you might sit with me for the service."

My eyes opened wide. Surely the countess would hate that, and I didn't want to cause a scene at his father's funeral.

Benedict seemed to understand my hesitation. "I'd planned something a bit more upbeat for our first date, but I'd really like your support today. In fact, it would mean the world."

What could I say? "Of course," I replied. "I'm right here."

We walked through the church together, and I felt everyone's eyes on me. The sensation prickled my skin. So far, Benedict and I had managed to keep our connection under wraps from the rest of the village. Now I was suddenly exposed. Even worse was the look on Evelyn Champney's face. She glared at me but said nothing. Thank goodness for that famous British decorum.

The Broomewode Choir took its place beside the pulpit. Vera looked very nervous, her shoulders hunched over like she was trying to make herself even smaller than usual. Once everyone was seated, the choirmaster, Hugo, cleared his throat. His salt-and-pepper hair was neatly parted to one side, and his square black glasses were pushed firmly against the bridge of his nose. At his nod, the choir launched into a haunting rendition of "How Lovely Are Thy Dwellings Fair," a piece I recognized solely from the movies.

The church was so beautiful inside, with its old stone and ancient pews. No doubt the Champneys had always sat at the front, though now it was their right as the grieving family.

The hymn finished, and the vicar asked us to sit. After welcoming everyone and explaining the order of service, he called upon Charles Radlier, the Master of the Hunt, for the first reading: "Holy Sonnet Number 10, by John Donne."

The church remained silent. No one stood.

I turned in the creaking pew to look for Charles and saw everyone else doing the same. Silent seconds passed. Benedict cleared his throat and leaned across to whisper to his mother. They seemed to exchange sharp words, the tone clear where the words were muffled. Finally, Lady Frome stood and, with great and pretty admirable elegance, walked to the pulpit. She leaned into the microphone and in a grave but clear voice recited, "Death be not proud, though some have called thee mighty and dreadful." She looked around at all of us. "For thou art not so."

She recited the poem brilliantly, elegant and composed. The countess certainly knew how to command attention. She finished on a strong note. "Death, thou shalt die."

"Well done, Mother," Benedict said beneath his breath. "Father would have been proud."

When Benedict gave his eulogy, I thought his father would have been even more proud. Standing beside the gleaming casket, Benedict reminded us that his father was never meant to be an earl. "He wasn't born, bred or trained for the responsibility. Yet he worked tirelessly to improve the estate." He spoke of his father's love of the land and the people. Looking at his mother, he said, "He was lucky in that he married the love of his life, and my mother and father were partners in everything." Here Lady Frome dabbed a lace handkerchief to her eye. "My father made mistakes, but he always meant well." Benedict turned to look at the casket. "'He was a man, take him for all in all, I shall not look upon his like again.'"

I felt a cold shiver go up my spine. He'd quoted Hamlet talking about his own father, the dead king. Did Benedict remember that Hamlet's father had also been murdered? And Hamlet himself wouldn't see the end of the play. I wished he'd chosen a different quote with which to end his eulogy.

CHAPTER 2

*W*hen the church service was over, the pallbearers, including Benedict, shouldered the casket for its short walk to the mausoleum. Evelyn Champney walked behind the coffin with her head bowed. Then we all followed and headed towards the family mausoleum for the burial. The rain had finally given up its reign, and a tentative sun pushed through the dispersing clouds. After the intensity of the church, the dim light and words of mourning, it was a relief to be out in the fresh air. The air was heating up. Late June in England can be warm or cool, but the day that had begun chilly was rapidly warming. I imagined there'd be some hot bodies in those black wool suits.

I spotted Florence in her operatic getup, walking slowly in impractical heels. Her handsome companion looked to be deep in conversation with another suave silver fox. I made my way over, determined to find out why she was so cozy with the countess.

"Poppy!" she exclaimed as I approached. "A sad day, my darling, a sad, sad day. How lucky Benedict is to have you by his side."

She air-kissed my cheeks. "You are a funny thing," she said quietly. I decided to ignore the comment about Benedict. I wasn't going to talk to anyone about our burgeoning romance—especially not Florence.

"I didn't realize you knew Lady Frome so well," I said, slowing my pace to match Florence's careful steps.

Florence asked if I could keep a secret. I had to stop myself from rolling my eyes; I felt like I was the Queen of Secrets. I nodded and she needed no urging to continue. She lowered her voice. "We're going into business together as soon as I win the competition. But I can't say more. It's top secret."

My thoughts jumbled each other so hard, it took a while for one to take precedence. Did Florence really think she was going to beat Hamish? That's what jumped out first. It wasn't going to be as easy as that. I kept quiet, musing as to why Florence was so certain of winning. Second, what kind of business was she cooking up? Did the grand Lady Evelyn Frome have theatrical ambitions? It was an unlikely alliance, though of course Florence was ambitious to the core. Getting close to the countess could definitely help her cause; I just wasn't clear exactly how. And the countess didn't strike me as someone who did anything without it benefiting herself.

Needless to say, I was burning with curiosity.

The ground was damp, and the scent of grass and soil filled the air. We were close to the mausoleum when I spotted a familiar sight. There was Mitty, the retired gamekeeper, holding on to Eve's arm. He looked a bit lost, as he'd been accustomed to Katie looking after him since he'd suffered a stroke. I was pleased he was well enough to attend the funeral. A selfish thought occurred to me. Was his mind sound enough for me to probe about the past? Mitty had dropped obscure hints about my mother. He'd been game-keeper at Broomewode the summer when Valerie, my birth mother, had worked at the hall. When she'd left Broome-wode, she'd been pregnant with me, but everything about that time, from why she abandoned me in front of a bakery to who my father was, remained a mystery.

Someone local had to remember something, and I was determined to engage Mitty in conversation if I could.

I excused myself from Florence and headed towards where Eve and Mitty had positioned themselves by the side of the mausoleum.

The mausoleum was an imposing building, its domed roof rising from the grounds around the church. Similar in style to Greek temples, the front was dominated by four ornate Doric columns and a grand set of stairs that led to the double doors of its entrance. It might be the fancy final resting place of earls and countesses, but it was still a graveyard.

As I approached, Eve was hushing Mitty—but he wasn't paying any attention. His voice was querulous and rising. He pointed at the casket now in front of the mausoleum. "That wasn't a natural death. I know it, and I won't stay quiet any longer. The viscount never died by accident."

My heart sank. Mitty was still as confused as ever. I touched them both lightly on the shoulder. "That's not the viscount," I said, feeling sorry for this old man who was losing his wits even as he recovered from his stroke. Obviously, it was affecting his mind more than anyone had realized. "It's the earl who was killed. He fell off his horse." I pointed to Benedict, standing beside the coffin. "See? The viscount's fine."

But to my surprise, Mitty waved me away, as if I was the confused one. "Not him. The other one." His voice was louder now, and a few heads turned. Including the countess, who was a few yards away, holding on to an older man's arm. Her head whipped round.

"Get that old lunatic out of here," she cried. "I won't have him making a mockery of my husband's funeral."

Eve bristled, and a murmur rippled through the crowd closest to Lady Frome.

"He's had a stroke, Mum," Benedict reminded her, again loud enough for everyone else to hear. "He's not recovered yet."

"This isn't a home for the mentally impaired," she retorted. "He needs proper care and nursing. I don't know why he's still here."

It was a terrible moment. No one knew what to say or do. Obviously, she was grieving, but her words were unbearably cruel. Couldn't she show some compassion to a man who'd worked for her family for years? For a kind old man who'd suffered a terrible trauma?

Mitty turned to me, clearly not understanding that the countess was trying to get rid of him. "Where's Katie?" he asked. "Why hasn't she come back yet?"

I looked into Mitty's blue eyes. So much soul shone through the worry. His white hair was groomed back with pomade, and his cheeks were pink from the fresh air. A rush of compassion went through me, and as I struggled to find the words to explain why Katie wasn't here, Edward stepped in, Lauren by his side. "Hello, old chap," he said. "Slipping away from me to flirt with the ladies, are you? Must say I can't blame you. Our Poppy is a great beauty."

At the sight of Edward, Mitty visibly relaxed. He'd been staying with Edward in his old, now-renovated, cottage since Katie's arrest.

Eve and I shared a look that communicated our joint worry. Why was Mitty talking about the dead viscount? Why was he trapped in that moment from the past?

"I guess the funeral was too much for him, after all," Eve whispered. "It's bringing old, painful memories to the surface again. The last person buried in the family tomb was the young viscount. Ever so sad it was. Stephen Champney fell off his horse, too; that's what's confused him. Stephen was Robert's second cousin. It was through Stephen dying that Robert became the next in line to the earldom."

"Why don't we head home and Lauren will make us a cup of tea?" Edward suggested. Mitty nodded, looking as confused as ever, and the three of them walked away.

My chest burned, like I'd eaten a plate of hot chilies. I put a hand to my chest. My heart was beating double-time. It was like my chest had been scorched from the inside. Strangely, though, the sensation wasn't unpleasant. It was a soothing warmth. Argh. This was confusing: I was supposed to be in tune with my body, but it seemed to be acting of its own accord.

I cast my eyes around the graveyard. Some instinct had alerted me. And then there, yes—a flash of blond hair by a crumbling gravestone. There were so many people milling around that I'd have missed the woman if she wasn't crouching down as though trying to stay out of sight. I felt another strong pull of recognition. Was it? Could it be? I squinted. Joanna? I stood on tiptoes, holding my breath, trying to contain the hope that was bubbling wildly within me. The woman was too far away for me to be sure. But I could *feel* her. I turned to Eve to see if she could tell if it was Joanna or not, but when I looked back again, the woman was gone. There was just a crumbling gravestone covered in ivy. Was my mind playing tricks on me or had she somehow melted away? Argh. Joanna. What was all this about?

"You okay, luvvie?" Eve whispered.

"Did you feel that?"

She looked at me quizzically. "Feel what?"

I sighed. "I swear I felt Joanna. She was close. I'm certain of it."

Eve looked pensive, like she was mulling something over. "Are you sure?" she asked, playing with the end of her long braid.

I had been. Now she was making me doubt myself. Probably, like Mitty, I was getting overwhelmed and a little confused.

Now the time had come to put the earl inside the mausoleum. The old door was opened with great solemnity. And the sound of knocking and cursing emerged from its depths. It was bizarre. I took a quick step forward, speaking without thinking, "There's someone trapped inside." The voice was male and so clear to me, I was astounded no one else was rushing forward to help.

An array of surprised and perplexed expressions turned my way, and suddenly panic took over. Was it a ghost I was

23

hearing? *Oh, way to go, Poppy. Reveal that you can commune with the dead at a public funeral.*

"I don't hear anything, Poppy," Eve said gently.

"You're imagining things, dear," a voice from across the crowd shouted.

Embarrassment prickled at the very edges of me. But to my surprise, DI Hembly made his way to the entrance of the mausoleum. Had he heard what I had? Surely I couldn't be the only one...unless it really was an angry ghost. I groaned. Angry ghosts were the worst: petulant, aggrieved, and very uncooperative. Talking with one of those was like dealing with a toddler tantrum over not wanting to leave the playground. I didn't think I had the patience today.

Hembly cleared his throat and then asked the vicar if they could pause the burial for a moment so they could check. The vicar looked completely bemused. He turned to Benedict for consent. To my relief, Benedict nodded, but his expression was hard to read. Did he think I was crazy and was simply placating me? Or did he trust me enough to simply go with the crazy? I had to hope it was the latter. One thing I knew for sure was that I was interrupting his dad's funeral, which was so not going to endear me to his haughty mom.

The countess was audibly sighing and rolling her eyes. But Hembly took no heed. He motioned for Sergeant Lane and I to come forward.

"Let's take a quick look," Hembly said. "Poppy, I trust your gut. Will you and your supersonic hearing lead the way?"

My trusted gut now turned somersaults. I looked at the imposing stairs that led to the entrance. He wanted me to go first? Great. I breathed in and out a few times, and before I could back out, a decidedly crude curse rumbled somewhere from the mausoleum's depths. Hembly and Lane didn't blink. So I *was* the only one hearing this nonstop tirade of frustration. And now I'd made the police aware of the problem. I stepped forward and hoped beyond hope that my acting skills were worthy enough that I could pretend there wasn't a ghost floating around.

CHAPTER 3

*H*eart in my mouth, I carefully climbed the steps to where the old door was already ajar. All my senses were tingling.

But on entering the mausoleum, I was taken aback by its beauty. It was crafted from the same golden Somerset stone as the rest of Broomewode and the surrounding villages, and the burgeoning sunlight from two panes of curved glass in the domed ceiling cast patterns of warm peach and yellow light on the walls. Thousands of hours must have gone into building this place. A labor of love for those who had died.

There was a staircase, which I figured led down to the crypt. I'd never encountered a crypt before and wasn't sure what to expect. The whole idea was pretty creepy, though. I mean, exploring an underground lair that could hold generations of deceased family members wasn't exactly how I usually spent a Friday morning, especially as the dead were often pretty active around me. But I did appreciate the planning that had gone into providing a place of rest for the dearly departed. Having seen ghosts all my life, I wasn't afraid of what was waiting for me once this life was over, but I knew not everyone felt that way.

I turned and motioned for Hembly and Lane to follow me. "Down here," I said in the most nonchalant voice I could muster. They both nodded solemnly. At least they didn't think I was cracking up. Hembly had a fresh buzz cut, silver streaks visible in the softer gray. His square jaw was set with a determined look.

As we descended the flight of steps, the atmosphere dramatically changed. All the beauty of upstairs slipped away with each step I took. The smell hit me first. Dank and musty, like wet stone. It was far colder than outside, and it felt as if every hair on my body was now standing to attention, alert and on the defense. It was dark, but the stairs were illuminated by a series of dim electric lightbulbs—which also showed up the thick layer of dust on the wall, though I could see some areas where the dust had rubbed off; presumably someone had come down here to make sure all was ready for the earl. As my eyes grew accustomed to the dim light, I spotted cobwebs in every possible corner, dark unmoving smudges where spiders lay in wait. I shivered. Ghosts I could deal with, but spiders gave me the absolute heebie-jeebies.

I wished Gerry were here. If I had to deal with ghosts, it would be nice to have a friendly one to lead the way. But Gerry's movements were restricted to the competition tent where he'd died and the inn. He'd managed to expand his range a bit but definitely not this far.

"You okay, Poppy?" Sergeant Lane whispered from behind me.

I nodded, not trusting myself to turn around for fear he'd see the trepidation on my face.

Let's go, Pops. You've faced far worse than a creepy old crypt.

The farther down we went, the louder the knocking became. It was so insistent, the sound echoing and angry, like someone locked out of their own front door, that I doubled my steps, racing down, no longer afraid of what I was about to discover, just determined to find whoever was down there and why they were so frustrated.

The last step dropped me straight into the heart of the crypt. It was cold and dim. I blinked a few times, hoping my eyes would adjust, but I could only make out shadows.

"Ah, damn this blasted thing!" someone shouted. It was a plummy, rich-toned voice. It was familiar to me, but I couldn't place it. "Let me out!"

Hembly used the flashlight on his phone and swept it across the room, illuminating its vast space. It was so much bigger than I'd imagined. The crypt was vaulted with openings for at least thirty coffins. The full scale of Broomewode's history hit me then. It was like time had lost its linear quality. So many generations stretching back; so many ahead of us. A wave of dizziness rolled over me, and I had to steady myself.

"Will you kindly restrain yourself?" another voice called out. "You're getting on my nerves."

I glanced around, but there was no one there—dead or alive.

Hembly and Lane were silent, their faces pale blue from the phone's torch, looking at me expectantly, waiting for an explanation for this unusual escapade. All I could hear was the beat of my own heart and then another round of huffing and puffing and knocking and banging—the tone increasingly exasperated, growing in intensity.

"Let me out of here!" the voice screeched again. "I know

you're there. I can hear you. You won't get away with this."

Neither DI Hembly nor Sergeant Lane made any sort of reaction. So it definitely was a ghost. My hearing was not supersonic, but I could see and hear the dead. Lucky me. And I so was not about to admit that to the police. If a ghost flashed past me, I was going to have to think fast.

My quick reflexes were tested when an elegant woman in a nightgown, her long gray hair under a nightcap, floated toward me. "My dear child," she said to me, "can you make that dreadful man stop? He's driving us all mad."

"Sir," Lane said quietly, pulling on the lapel of his dark suit. "Something doesn't feel right down here. It's so cold, so much colder than just a moment ago."

"Oh, thank heavens," I said under my breath. The relief of knowing I wasn't the only one attuned to the habits of the recently departed was immense.

"Nonsense," Hembly called back. "You're just spooked, Lane. Pull yourself together. Let's have a look around."

"What are you saying, Elizabeth? Who's there?" An autocratic-looking man in a red Army uniform with a dress sword by his side, stepped out of the shadows to stand by the woman in the nightgown. Oh, this was fun. I was fairly certain I'd seen him in one of the portraits lining the walls of Broomewode Hall. He looked down at me. "Well, don't just stand there, girl. Take that dreadful commoner away. He's not one of the family and his manners are appalling. The language he uses in front of the ladies is not to be borne."

As we stepped deeper into the crypt, the noise started up again. The sound was unbearable. So much anguish and frustration. Lane located a light switch, and a dim bulb flickered overhead.

Despite the cool of the crypt, sweat began to gather at the base of my spine. There was definitely someone trapped inside a coffin. Which was strange, and for the first time, I wondered if they could be alive. Every ghost I knew could travel through matter. In fact, thinking of Gerry, I wished sometimes they weren't so good at walking through walls and locked doors!

"Get me out of here," the voice screeched. "It's too heavy. This thing won't lift."

"I'm sure I heard something, but it's so dark in here," I said. As I'd hoped, the resident ghosts were only too happy to lead me to a wooden coffin lying on the stone floor.

"Who's there? Release me this second," the ghost commanded.

I was smart enough not to attempt it on my own.

"Over here," I called. Sergeant Lane looked at me and then the coffin, the alarm clear in his face, but raced over anyway.

"There's something in there?"

"I'm not sure. I thought I heard a noise." It sounded lame, but I didn't want to tell them I heard someone yelling in there. Not when they heard nothing. I was going to have a big enough job explaining myself as it was. Why hadn't I kept my mouth shut? Normally, I was better at controlling myself, but the funeral, Mitty's outburst, glimpsing Joanna, it had all rattled me out of my usual caution.

DI Hembly came over, and they both shone their torches on the lid. "Been tampered with," Hembly said. Now I saw what he meant. There were scratches that were obviously new, and the dust wiped off around the edges. The lid didn't seem to be sitting right, either. I shuddered.

"Get me out of here. Get me out of here," the ghost wailed.

"Yes, please do what you can to release that man," the genteel lady said to me. "He's really becoming rather tiresome."

The men lifted the lid of the coffin, and as I'd feared, out stormed an irate ghost, floating into the air and turning round to look right at me, just as surprised as I was. I gasped. It was Charles Radlier, the Master of the Hunt! No wonder he didn't turn up to the funeral to read the poem—he was dead himself!

"What on earth is all this?" he asked, furious. "Am I bloody dead?"

"Yes, you ruddy well are," said the military man. "And if you can't mind your language in front of the ladies, you can clear off."

I opened my mouth, then shut it again. I was desperate to calm everyone down, explain what had happened, and then ask him who his murderer was, but how could I do that with the two officers right next to me?

While I was seeing ghosts, the officers were pretty surprised to find the body of Charles Radlier, freshly dead.

"You," I began, but to my horror, Charles began to flicker. "Who murdered you?" I cried out, desperate to commune with the ghost before he crossed over to the other side. But it was too late. Charles Radlier vanished.

"Yes. Good question, Poppy," DI Hembly said, obviously thinking I'd been speaking to the corpse.

I looked down. Charles's body had been laid on top of its previous resident.

They thought I was talking to the corpse.

Then, as though my morning wasn't stressful enough, a second ghost floated up from the coffin. He was quite a young man, with mutton chop whiskers, wearing a black suit that had seen better days. "What did you do that for?" he asked in a mournful tone.

"You were holding him against his will," the stern military man said. I bet he was a colonel or something high up. He definitely had the habit of command.

"At least he was company for me. You never let me join in your card games or discussions. You treat me as though I do not exist."

I couldn't believe I was in the middle of a ghostly dorm room squabble.

"You shouldn't even be here," the colonel said. I'd decided he must be a colonel. Or a general, maybe. I wasn't too up on British military terms.

"I'm a Champney just as much as you are."

"Certainly not. You were the base-born child of a second son."

"We share the same blood," the man with the mutton chops said, then looked down at his ghostly form. "Or we did. In life."

"Really, Cyril, I do think Charles has a point." The lady in the nightdress smiled at the ghost kindly. "Are you perchance proficient at whist?"

The young man rubbed his hands gleefully. "I've always been partial to cards."

"How did you know?" Sergeant Lane asked, shaking his head and looking at me.

I gulped. I'd been too busy trying to find the ghost to think of a good reason why I'd known he was down here in the first place. I went as close to the truth as I could. "I have exceptional hearing," I told them. Understatement of the year. "I heard something. I'm not sure what."

"Well, good thing you did. Now we can let this poor man's family know what's become of him."

But what had happened to poor Charles Radlier? The man wasn't exactly likable, but being dumped in another person's coffin? That was low. And being placed on top of another spirit's body, or in this case the skeleton of a former Charles, who was lonely for a friend, was like a magnet holding him back.

I looked at the ghosts and said, "Wouldn't it be nice if the walls could talk and tell us what happened?"

They glanced at each other. "I was outside in the moon-light, reciting The Charge of the Light Brigade to Elizabeth," the military man said. "When we returned, that blighter was ranting to be let out."

Okay, it had happened at night. One very vague clue. "Do you think it happened very recently?" I asked, again, staring at my ghost companions.

"Time loses meaning after a while, dear," the woman I assumed was Elizabeth said.

DI Hembly answered as though I'd asked him the ques-tion. "I'd say it happened while they were preparing the crypt for the earl. This man hasn't been dead too long. We'll get the forensics team down here." He played his cell phone flash-light over Charles Radlier's body. "Not much doubt as to how he died. The back of his head's been bashed in." He looked back. "Any sign of a murder weapon?"

We all glanced around the dim space.

The military man harrumphed. "No doubt they'll find it

in their own time, but I would point out there are some tools kept in that chest over there. They might want to inspect the hammer."

"Yes," said Charles, the young man in the black suit. How confusing that both he and the recently dead man were named Charles. "And I can tell you it was a terrible shock when I came back from church and found the lid off my coffin. One likes a little privacy." I stared at him, and he said, "I like to go to the church and sit in on the services. So nice to see the people, and listen to the hymns. This vicar's very good, I must say."

Wait, was he saying the lid of his coffin was off before Charles Radlier was killed? Then it was a premediated murder. And I couldn't tell the detectives that.

I could lead them to a pretty big clue, though, assuming the ghosts were right.

I wandered over to where they'd said there was a chest and found it easily, in a dusty corner. My mobile phone flashlight revealed more disturbed dust. Thank goodness. "Detective Hembly, I think you should see this," I said, then winced, realizing I'd parroted those words from TV mysteries.

DI Hembly didn't seem fazed that I was acting like one of his junior detectives. He walked over and I pointed. "It looks as though this chest has been opened recently. The dust's been disturbed."

He nodded and, pulling out gloves from his suit pocket and donning them, opened the lid.

Sergeant Lane looked over his shoulder. I was feeling a little claustrophobic as all the ghosts had come close to peer into the chest too. "I'd say that hammer looks about the right shape to have done the job," Sergeant Lane said.

"As I've already explained," the military ghost said.

DI Hembly carefully replaced the lid of the chest and the detectives walked back to the coffin. "Looks as though he was killed here in the crypt, then," DI Hembly said.

"By someone who knew there was a chest of tools down here?" Sergeant Lane suggested.

"Or they brought the hammer with them, and found the perfect place to hide it."

"I don't know, sir. I think it was all planned out before-hand," Sergeant Lane said.

The military man nodded. "I like this young man. He's got potential."

I hid a smile as Sergeant Lane continued. "Somehow, Charles Radlier was lured down here, then, when his back was turned, his assailant struck the back of his head with the hammer." He mimed the action against the Detective Inspector. Then he peered into the coffin. "How tall a man was Charles Radlier? The killer would have had to be very tall to bring the hammer down with enough force to kill him."

DI Hembly looked thoughtful. "Unless Mr. Radlier was bending over at the time of the assault." He leaned over the coffin. "Perhaps peering at the coffin for some reason."

I couldn't keep silent any longer. They were so close. "What if the coffin was already open? That would make anyone stop and look. And then, when they were struck, they might tumble in."

Both detectives nodded. "Certainly possible," DI Hembly said. "Which means your assailant no longer needs to be very tall. Or even especially strong." He turned to me. "Why, Poppy could have done it."

"But I didn't," I said, backing away in alarm.

"LET'S get Poppy some fresh air and some hot coffee. We need to stop the earl's funeral and section off the crypt as a crime scene."

"Yes, sir. I'll call it in as soon as we're above ground."

"Come again and visit us, dear. We don't get many visitors," Elizabeth said.

I smiled at her, though I really doubted I'd be coming down here to make up a foursome for whist.

As I walked back to the staircase, a strange sensation came over me, and my body temperature changed. I couldn't tell if it was warmer or colder. It was more like my blood was flowing differently, my skin tingling. I followed the feeling and found myself at the edge of another vault. This one was in a more prominent position, and the coffin had elaborate brass piping around its edges and a glossy walnut finish. I squinted at the name in the half light. Stephen Champney. Robert's cousin who'd crashed to his death in a terrible horse-riding accident. I ran my fingers along the inscription and felt a well of sadness. He was only my age when he died. Mitty's words echoed in my head. He sounded so convinced that the viscount's death wasn't an accident.

But why? I shook my head. How sad to die so young. How different Broomewode Village might be now if he had lived and Robert Champney had never inherited the earldom.

Elizabeth floated over to where I had my hand on the coffin. "He's a nice young lad. You'd like him. A little remote, though. Keeps himself to himself."

"Thinks he's better than us," the military man announced.

"Nonsense, Cyril. He's shy."

I'd have liked to meet Stephen Champney and ask him about the past, but he seemed to be elsewhere.

As I came back out into the group of mourners, I nearly turned tail and went back down again. Communing with the dead had its downside, but I'd never felt quite so horrified by my "gift." Thanks to me, the earl's funeral would have to be postponed, and a lot of mourners were going to be looking at me and wondering how I'd known a murdered man was in the crypt.

I hoped I would not be the next person to need a good lawyer.

BACK ABOVE GROUND, no one seemed to know what to do. The vicar stood beside the coffin as though to protect it from embarrassment. Evelyn Champney looked at me as though I'd single-handedly ruined the funeral of her husband, the earl. Which, come to think of it, I had. The cold sharpness of her gaze promised that she would never forgive me.

I hastily glanced away. Benedict didn't look angry with me, but he wasn't happy. I almost wished I'd kept my mouth shut. Then I thought of Charles Radlier's family, wondering what had happened to him. As someone whose life had been clouded by mystery, I knew how damaging it could be not to know what had happened to people you loved.

DI Hembly explained that the funeral was going to have to be paused as the mausoleum was now a crime scene. He had a commanding air, but even so, a man strode forward and began to argue. I didn't know who this man was, but he had an air of authority. DI Hembly took him aside, and they spoke quietly, then the man returned and had a few quiet words with Benedict and then with Evelyn Champney. The countess began to cry, and my cheeks flushed red. I burned with shame. These people were here to mourn and say their goodbyes, and now I'd interrupted the funeral—and everyone knew it.

Florence pulled the countess to her bosom and began to murmur in her ear. I was grateful that my former baking competitor was there to comfort her new business partner, but how like Florence to position herself in the center of the drama. It wasn't like she was the mothering kind.

But it wasn't Florence I cared about.

I stepped into the crowd, desperate to find Benedict and explain what had happened as best as I could. I couldn't bear the idea he would hold me responsible for sabotaging his father's funeral. I finally caught sight of Benedict to the right of the mausoleum, talking earnestly with the vicar. As I approached them, I caught the end of their conversation arranging for the earl to be removed by the undertakers. Benedict glanced at me, then looked away.

What had I done?

But just then a voice said, "You're not to worry, child. You did the right thing."

With a jolt, I felt certain the voice belonged to my dad. Or the ghost of my father. Where had it come from? I spun round, looking for another ghost, this one much more dear to me. But there was no one. Nothing. For the second time that day, a person from my past had suddenly appeared and then vanished.

CHAPTER 4

The funeral was clearly over. I decided to collect Gateau and head back to the inn. I didn't know where else to go. People were milling around confused. There'd been a funeral reception planned at the hall, and I imagined many of the guests had been invited back anyway since they were here and the food had already been prepared.

However, no one had invited me.

It had been Eve's idea to book my old room (or what I considered to be my old room!) for the evening, knowing I'd be here for the funeral and wouldn't want to drive home and back again in the morning. It was such a comfort to know that if the room didn't rent for the weekend, it was mine for the night without charge. I slept well at the inn, though my dreams were wilder, more intense, littered with images of hawks and rippling water, snippets of the lullaby I heard Katie Donegal sing, flashes of all the faces I'd encountered in Broomewode over the weeks. Dead and alive. As frightening as it could be, it felt like clues to my past were swirling around in my subconscious, and there was something weirdly comforting about it.

Elspeth and Jonathon caught up with me, and with relief I told them everything that had happened. Elspeth nodded. "We thought it must be something like that."

I was so upset, I was close to tears. "I ruined the earl's funeral. I wish I'd kept my mouth shut." People were casting me odd glances as they chatted in groups or headed for cars.

"You did the right thing," Elspeth assured me, echoing what the ghost I thought was my father had said. It did help, as I considered Elspeth a grandmotherly figure. Still, I felt raw with humiliation.

"Yes. That dead bloke will get a proper burial, and hopefully the police will figure out who killed him," Jonathon added. Then he glanced at Elspeth. "We must get off to the tent. Lots to do for the final weekend of filming."

They left together.

I found Gateau with Eve, and she also had consoling words for me, understanding at once how the morning had upset me. "Have you checked your phone? I let Ruta know that the funeral's been postponed, and she wants you back ASAP, as they're likely to get an early lunch rush now. Probably the last thing you feel like is work, I know, but it does help take your mind off your troubles."

I sighed. Eve was right, and I wasn't about to let Ruta down. I'd switched my phone off before the funeral and was in no hurry to turn it on and come back into the world again. We headed back to the inn together, and Eve, like Elspeth and Jonathon, listened to my story and confirmed I'd done the right thing. Thank goodness for my coven. I didn't know what I'd do without their support and advice.

Discovering Charles Radlier's ghost and then his body laid on top of a skeleton had given me quite the fright. I knew from my witch sisters that Broomewode was an energy vortex that drew witches. Elspeth had told me it was a good place for me to learn my craft.

Broomewode had drawn me first when I suspected a link with my birth mother. I couldn't have imagined all I'd find when I got here—powers I hadn't known I possessed, a coven of other witches who welcomed me so I finally stopped feeling like there was something wrong with me. Unfortunately, there were dark forces here as well. And I seemed to keep bumping into them.

Back at the inn, I slipped upstairs to change out of Gina's black dress. It was itching under the arms, and I couldn't wait to get back into my comfortable work clothes.

But of course, life couldn't be straightforward.

Floating inside my room was Gerry. Cars-and-trucks shirt, spiky reddish hair, ruddy skin. His attention was fixed on a vase of pale pink roses, or more accurately, lifting each rose from the water with his ghostly powers and letting them hover. He was definitely improving his poltergeist abilities.

I cleared my throat, as he'd been so busy concentrating on his trick, he hadn't heard me come in.

Gerry spun round. "Pops! What you doing back already?"

Gateau jumped out of my arms immediately, hissing and arching her back. There was no love lost between these two.

"The funeral was canceled."

"What? Tell me all about it." He threw himself on the bed and patted the other side. I wanted to be alone. But Gerry didn't understand the meaning of personal space. I didn't move.

"Now, Pops, I know what you're going to say. You're going to say—" He cleared his throat and then, in a voice that sounded impressively like mine—except more whiny—said, "'Stop hanging out in my room uninvited,' but I didn't know you'd be back so soon. And did you see how well I did with the roses? Eve put them there, by the way. She seems like she's very fond of you."

That was nice of her.

Oh, Gerry. How I loved to hate his intrusions, but he did make me laugh, and he was very good at eavesdropping and getting information that was useful, for instance in a murder investigation. Gateau raced to her favorite armchair and jumped up, curling up so her butt faced Gerry.

"Gerry," I began, but he held up his hand.

"Okay. I know already. News travels fast in Broomewode. Turns out you created quite the scene at the earl's funeral. I thought you might be in hiding somewhere, on account of the gossip."

My heart sank, lower and heavier than ever before. "I was trying to do the right thing," I said. "I knew there was a ghost down there. I could hear him cursing and trying to get out of the coffin. I only wish that it hadn't turned the funeral plans upside down."

To my surprise, Gerry floated over to make more room when I'd flopped on the bed in despair.

"You did the right thing," he said. "How could you ignore a poor ghost in distress?" He put an arm around me, or at least, attempted to. I thanked him for his kindness. Then he looked upset. "After you freed him from his coffin, did he, you know?" He made a motion with his hands flying up toward the ceiling.

I nodded. Poor Gerry. Most ghosts passed over with little trouble. Why was he still here?

"I'll banish myself to the pub downstairs so you can get ready for work in peace. And give that little monster a break." He gestured at Gateau, who flicked her tail at him without turning.

I was amazed that I didn't have to throw Gerry out of my room myself. Was it possible that he was actually maturing?

He bade me a "Fond farewell, dearest Poppy" in his best impression of the aristocracy and floated through the door. I gave it a beat or two, just to make sure he really was gone, before unzipping my dress. I wished I could run a bath and soak the morning's stress away, but Ruta needed me.

I opened the closet and saw the pretty summer dress I'd brought along with me for the weekend. It *was* the final weekend of the baking competition, after all, and past contestants were due for a final on-camera interview. It was a gorgeous number, knee-length and white with a sweetheart neckline and duck-egg-blue trim. When I put it on, I felt like a 1930s starlet. But alas, that feeling would have to wait. There was work to do.

No doubt I'd hoped to wow Benedict in that dress too, but it didn't look like that would happen. After I'd ruined his father's funeral, I doubted Ben was looking forward to seeing me anytime soon, and his mother would probably bar the doors of Broomewode Hall against me.

I changed quickly into work clothes, pulling back my hair. With Gerry gone, Gateau had promptly fallen asleep, like the true lady of leisure she was.

I descended the stairs and made my way to the kitchen. We'd expected a busier than normal day, as it was the earl's funeral, but none of us had anticipated it being quite this early.

I expected to see Ruta running around the kitchen at high speed, but she greeted me with a wave, her expression calm.

"Heard about what happened at the funeral," she said in a tone I couldn't quite place. Was it soft? Surprised? It certainly wasn't gossipy, and for that I was thankful. "Did you really hear something in the crypt?"

I'd had some time to think of a slightly plausible explanation. "Well, the door to the mausoleum was open, of course, to receive the earl. Something must have fallen inside and I was standing in the exact spot to hear it. I have good hearing," I said, trying to shrug the whole thing off.

"Maybe you're in the wrong business," she said. "Got the detective's bug. Or maybe just an eye on a detective?" She shot me a knowing look.

Don't get me wrong. I'd noticed that Adam Lane was a hot guy with dimples. Kind and thoughtful, too, with a steady job. But my affection lay elsewhere. Sadly. It would be far less complicated to crush on Sgt. Lane.

Before Ruta could tease me any more, Pavel walked in, struggling under the weight of a box of carrots. He heaved it onto the work surface, grimacing. "Someone thought it would be a good idea to make carrot souffles," he said, raising his eyebrows. "I mean, have you heard of anything more ridiculous?"

Ruta laughed. It would take a lot more than a slight about carrots to penetrate her thick skin.

"Never had one myself," I admitted, "but if Ruta likes them, then they've got to be good."

"Thank you, Poppy," Ruta replied. "At least someone round here trusts my direction."

While Pavel set about peeling a seemingly endless stack of carrots, I asked Ruta where I'd be most helpful. "I can give you a hand with the specials. I'm ahead of schedule."

But, as ever, Ruta told me she had everything under control—I was just there for backup if lunch was crazy. I got on with my dough for tomorrow and tried to put the morning's events out of my mind. I desperately wanted to know why and how Charles Radlier had ended up in someone else's coffin that morning. But I had to stay professional. Keep it simple, allow myself to go through the motions, head down. Flour, sugar, butter—all carefully weighed out on my electric scales. Switch on the mixer; find my favorite whisk, which Gerry loved to move around.

Ruta turned up the radio, and we worked in peaceful synchronicity, a pop tune I didn't recognize floating through the kitchen.

I was so immersed in my work that I didn't notice the inn's new waitress, Philly, until she loudly cleared her throat. Her hair was falling out of its bun, and she looked harried.

"Sorry to ask, but we're slammed. Any chance someone can help me serve in the pub?"

Ruta gazed over at Pavel—painfully shy Pavel, who had trouble looking women in the eye—and then turned to me. "Poppy? Would you mind? You're ahead of schedule, and we're fine in here for now."

I smiled and agreed immediately. I was more than happy to go. This way I could eavesdrop on what everyone was saying about the funeral and Charles Radlier's murder. With luck, Gerry was out there on the same errand and we could compare notes later.

Philly passed me a fresh apron, and I retied my hair. I wasn't the most experienced waitress, but I could offer a willing pair of hands. And a sneakily open pair of ears.

I pushed open the door to the pub, and the noise hit me. The place was packed, and everyone seemed to be talking at once.

A lot of people from the funeral had come to the pub and were having a drink at the bar. I wondered if some of them had been invited back to Broomewode Hall and chosen the pub instead. Or maybe Evelyn Champney had shut the doors on everyone. I hoped most of the funeral food could be frozen and reheated.

As Philly ran through the table numbers with me, gossip and speculation flooded the room. It was noisy, boisterous even. Certainly not a wake; but it wasn't even close to being somber. Now that the villagers and Londoners were away from the church, they were letting rip with their opinions. I heard snippets: Who were Charles's enemies? Did anyone have motive to murder him? Why was he hidden in the crypt, of all places?

And then I saw Hamish and Florence. They were sitting together at a small, round oak table by the window. Florence's chestnut curls cascaded down her back. She was sipping a cappuccino, Hamish, an espresso. No alcohol for these two competitors and apparently no talking either. Even from here, I could feel the coolness between them. It was understandable. One of them would win the competition on Sunday, and the other would have come all this way to be runner-up. But I knew that both Hamish and Florence wouldn't think of it as second place—to them, it would be losing.

"That's for your friends," Philly whispered, rolling her eyes. She handed me a jug of iced lemon water. "The woman asked for this." Ha. Trust Florence to request fancy water when the bar was so busy.

I carried over the jug and set it down on the table. Up close, I could see Florence was looking incredibly smug. I didn't even want to know why.

"Oh, darling, have they roped you into delivering drinks now? How ghastly," Florence said. "You should put your foot down and tell them you're not a waitress."

"I'm happy to help, actually. It's nice to lend a hand when someone needs it."

A loud wheezing came from the next table. I turned and saw Edward, Lauren, and Mitty sitting together. Mitty still looked upset. He seemed to be having a coughing fit. Edward handed him a glass of water, and the old man drank deeply. His coughing subsided. I sighed with relief. That poor man had been through enough.

I turned back to Florence. "How is the countess? I feel terrible about the whole morning."

"I put her to bed, poor darling," Florence said. "What a terrible shock she's had."

Now it was Hamish's turn to cough, but this time it was in surprise. For my part, I was glad I'd already set the jug of water down, otherwise it might have ended up in Florence's lap. Out of shock or spite...well, we'd never know.

"Are you that close?" I asked, trying hard to keep the incredulity out of my tone but failing miserably.

Florence looked around, flicked her curls over her

shoulder and then lowered her voice. "I shouldn't tell you this, but you're both my friends and I know you'll be thrilled for me."

She paused dramatically, clearly waiting for one of us to urge her to continue. I didn't want to play into Florence's performance, but I was curious. "Go on," I said.

"Well, Evelyn and I are going to have our own television series. Isn't that exciting? The handsome man with me today? I'm sure you noticed him, Poppy. He's going to be the executive producer." Her eyes sparkled and her skin glowed, and Florence looked thoroughly pleased with herself. But I couldn't share Florence's enthusiasm. A man had just been discovered murdered. She was dressed all in black from attending the failed funeral of another murdered man. And yet all Florence could think about was her exciting career prospects. I didn't know why I was surprised.

"I thought you said no one wanted a TV show starring a runner-up," I said, remembering what she'd said the week before, how desperately she'd wanted to win so her film and TV career could flourish.

To add insult to injury, Florence leaned over and patted Hamish's hand. "Please don't take this the wrong way, but we all know I'm going to win this weekend."

I felt my jaw drop open. Surely Florence didn't really think it was in the bag?

Hamish sharply pulled his hand away. "No," he said quietly but firmly. "We don't all know that."

She let out a tinkling laugh. "I'm so happy to see you holding on to your morale. You barely made it this far. You should be proud of yourself."

Patronizing much? Hamish looked as though he had a few things he'd like to say, but he pressed his lips shut.

"Anyway, I've had a few private meetings with Evelyn." It irked me every time she used Lady Frome's first name, as though they were BFFs. She glanced up under her lashes at me. "And Benedict, of course. I'll be the presenter, and the series will be about Broomewode Hall, its history of entertaining, and Evelyn and I will cook famous local recipes. It's going to be so quaint. The only downside is that I'll have to be away from London during filming. I'm not sure how I'll survive as a country bumpkin." She laughed softly. "But at least I'll see lots of you, Poppy. Perhaps I can even find you a job on set."

Lucky me.

I was gobsmacked, as the British like to say. Absolutely gobsmacked. Gerry floated into view, frowning. "Well, well, well. Someone has let their minor success on a baking show go to their head." He rolled his eyes and then turned a somersault to emphasize his point. "Florence sounds totally fame-hungry."

This time it was easy to ignore Gerry's ghostly commentary. I was having trouble focusing on anything but the way she'd looked at me when she said Benedict had been in the meetings. Why hadn't he said anything to me? As though reading my thoughts, Florence said, "Ben's got some wonderful ideas. I've told him I'll create a special Eggs Benedict for him." She laughed again.

Now he was 'Ben.'

Hamish said, "You angling to be the next countess?" The Scottish police officer wasn't one to beat about the bush.

She laughed again. "And what if I am?"

Hamish frowned and leaned in closer. "Because Benedict's fallen for Poppy, and you know it."

I felt warm inside that Hamish had noticed. But Florence only tossed her hair again, a trait that was beginning to fiercely irritate me.

"If he has," Florence said, shrugging, "then Poppy has nothing to worry about."

Her real thoughts were left unsaid, but they lay floating in the air like poison gas. Clearly Florence took it for granted that if she put any effort into stealing Benedict away, he'd be hers.

I hadn't even had my first date with Benedict yet, and now I had royally messed up his father's funeral. I had a depressing feeling she might be right.

CHAPTER 5

$\mathcal{W}$hen Philly called me over, I was thankful to be able to excuse myself from the table. Florence had unnerved me. Gerry was still loitering as I returned to the bar, so I whispered a request for him to spy for me. "See what the villagers are speculating." He saluted, also happy to be put to work. I had to admit, sometimes it was nice having Gerry around. And useful.

Before he drifted off, he said, glancing at the smug-looking Florence and the depressed-looking Hamish, "I wish I could go as far as Broomewode Hall. I'd like to join those meetings of hers myself. I'm sure she's lying. I know where I'd like to shove her Eggs Benedict."

I appreciated the support. I might end up baking Benedict and Florence's wedding cake one day, but at least I'd always have Gerry.

I joined Philly, and she showed me where the measures were kept for pouring wine by the glass. "They've started drinking early," she said in a conspiratorial tone. "Good news for us, bad news for their hangovers tomorrow." She flashed a grin. "The drink tickets come out here." She pointed to a small black machine positioned by the coffee machine. "They'll have the order and table number on them."

I nodded, trying to keep up. Eve was busy at the bar but shot me an encouraging smile.

I took the first ticket from the machine. "Two medium glasses of Chablis," I read aloud. "Okay, I can do that."

I removed the white wine glasses from the rack overhead and rummaged in the fridge for the Chablis. As I poured the measures, I scanned the room for the right table. Just my luck. It belonged to a table of posh Londoners—friends of the earl and countess I'd spotted at the funeral. I took a deep breath. Everyone there had witnessed my outburst, heard my cries that someone was in the crypt. Now I was going to have to face these strangers who'd already formed an opinion about me—no doubt a seriously negative one—and smile politely.

I walked over to the table slowly, eager to eavesdrop on the crowd.

"Money troubles. That's what I heard," someone was saying.

"Serious financial mismanagement," another voice said.

Both belonged to men, and then I realized that lots of people I'd seen at last week's hunt were here. Had Charles Radlier gotten himself into hot water with his finances and needed to borrow money? Did he accept an offer from the wrong people?

I arrived at the table and tried to smile at the couple in front of me. They were dressed in expensive-looking suits, hers made of inky blue silk, his jet-black, and both were groomed to within an inch of their lives. They simultane-ously tapped into their mobile phones, typing ferociously.

"Two glasses of Chablis?" I asked, hoping beyond hope they wouldn't ask me about my outburst at the funeral.

But I needn't have worried. The couple didn't even look up from their phones.

"That's right," the woman said, still staring into her screen. "Many thanks."

I set down the drinks, not sure whether to be grateful for the anonymity their rudeness afforded me or offended. I went back to the bar and helped Eve prepare some coffees.

"I've never seen it like this," Eve admitted. "It's like a New Year's Eve party, except everyone's dressed in black."

"Not very solemn, are they?"

"The earl wasn't the most popular of men. And it doesn't take a lot for people round here to latch on the newest piece of gossip. It's the village way."

I couldn't disagree with Eve, although I felt fiercely protective of Broomewode. Instead of brooding, I followed Eve's lead, and before I knew it, I was into the swing of things front of house. A big order for brandies came in, and I felt certain it belonged to a group from the hunt. I offered to take it over, eager to eavesdrop on their conversation.

Carefully carrying the tray of expensive cognac, I followed Philly's table map to a group of men in the corner. Unlike the rest of the room, their mood was more serious.

"The mausoleum presented a perfect place to hide the body where it would never be found," one of them said.

"If it hadn't been for that girl, whoever it was would have got away with murder."

"How did she know?" another man piped up.

I bowed my head, hoping to remain unnoticed as before. If I hadn't been a witch, the body would have stayed where it was and poor Charles's ghost would have remained trapped. I knew I'd done a good thing—I just couldn't admit to it. I put the drinks in front of the men and then hurried away without so much as a "here you go." I wasn't going to risk being recognized for the sake of being polite. I hoped the explanation I'd given Ruta would hold up. Someone was bound to put me on the spot soon.

On the way back to the bar, Sgt. Lane caught my eye and waved me over. I hadn't even noticed he was there. Lane was alone, writing in his notebook. I figured he was up to the same game as me, listening to what people said when they thought no one was listening. That could fill an entire book. A juicy bestseller at that.

I asked how he was doing, and Lane replied with a smile, dimples creasing. "I'm okay, but I feel for you having to be back at work so soon after what you experienced this morning."

"I could say the same for you."

He laughed. "I'm never really off the job."

Me too, although I couldn't explain why. It wasn't like I could switch off my witchy senses. I felt constantly on high alert.

I explained that I was getting used to nasty surprises. "I've already overheard some speculation that Charles Radlier was in financial trouble."

"Looks like your hearing is paying sleuthing dividends today, if you'll pardon the finance pun."

I laughed. "You're excused."

"But seriously, Poppy. I have to ask, how did you know the

dead man was down there?" Lane's eyes were open and warm. It wasn't an accusation, more like curiosity. And I certainly couldn't blame him for that. I wanted to know why my hearing had suddenly become so powerful, too.

"I thought I heard a noise," I said, knowing I sounded lame. I gave him the same story about the open door I'd given Ruta, but he didn't look as easily convinced.

Eve passed our table with a tray full of empty glasses and caught the tail end of our conversation. "It's the rats down there. I heard something as well. Terrible they are, fiendishly large."

I breathed a sigh of relief. I was so grateful to Eve for pretending she'd heard something too. Rats. Good one.

"Don't tell DI Hembly. He's terrified of rats."

I laughed, an image of Hembly climbing into one of the vaults to escape a rat flashing across my mind.

"Let's catch up later," he said, and I accompanied Eve back to the bar.

"Thank you so much," I said once we were out of earshot. "You really saved my bacon."

"He's a nice chap," Eve said, "and he means well. But the last thing the coven needs is attention from the police."

For the third time that day, shame flooded my body. Not only had my outburst ruined Benedict's father's funeral, but I'd put my sisters at risk, too. Sometimes being a witch was a heavy weight on my shoulders. I wasn't sure the advantages were worth the cost.

Eve laid a cool hand on my arm. "Stop beating yourself up, Pops. You did the right thing. Someone murdered that poor man and would have got away with it if it wasn't for you. Please be proud of your powers. I am."

"You're going to make me cry," I said, trying to sound jokey, but really I was overcome with emotion. Too much had happened too fast. I felt like things were spinning out of control.

"Oh, nonsense. You're made of sterner stuff. Now can you take these sandwiches over to Mitty and Edward?"

I took the plates, glad of an excuse to talk with Mitty again. I was very sorry Katie Donegal had to lie low, but now I could finally talk to Mitty properly. Even if his mind was a bit feeble, I was certain he might remember something about my birth parents...all I needed to do was land on the right line of questioning, find the right sequence of words.

When I arrived at the table, Mitty and Edward were deep in conversation, Mitty's tone insistent and rising in volume. He looked up as I set down the sandwiches. "Valerie will remember," he said, looking right at me.

I swallowed uncomfortably and couldn't stave off the disappointment. Mitty's mind wasn't on the mend.

"This is Poppy," Lauren said. "You remember Poppy."

Lauren smiled at me and then pulled her blond hair into a ponytail, preparing to delve into the gigantic roast chicken sandwich I'd delivered.

But Mitty paid no heed to Lauren. He continued on the same track, insisting that Valerie would understand what he was talking about. He looked at me, imploring. "I was nearby when the viscount went riding that day. I heard the shot. It was a rifle. I can recognize the sound anywhere. And it spooked the horse and sent Stephen Champney flying over the edge of the cliff. It was no accident. Somebody shot that gun on purpose."

He stopped and hung his head, addressing the rest of his

speech to the tabletop. "I never said anything. Should have. 'Fraid I'd lose the job. I had a family to provide for, and besides, the young lord was dead and it was impossible to prove what I heard. I didn't know who to turn to. You knew it, too. I'm sorry, Valerie."

"It's okay, matey," Edward said softly. "All that's in the past. And remember what we told you earlier? It's Robert Champney we tried to bury today. That's the funeral we attended. The viscount's cousin."

"Second cousin," Mitty said fiercely. "That's all he was, a second cousin. Never meant to be the heir. Robert Champney," Mitty repeated. "That's what I'm saying. That's the man I saw riding across the hills that day."

What was Mitty saying? "You saw the earl?" I said, slipping into the seat next to Mitty.

"Not the earl. Robert Champney," Mitty repeated. "You know, I was always suspicious of that man. He never told anyone he'd been riding the same fields as his cousin that day. But I know what I saw."

Did he? Mitty sounded so sure of himself, but he was mixing up names and times.

But Mitty wasn't finished talking. There was an urgency to his voice that set my mind racing.

"It was only later," he said, reaching towards me and taking my hands, "when the viscount's horse came back riderless, a search was mounted. That's when Stephen Champney was found, his body at the base of those terrible cliffs."

Cold dread spread through my stomach. What Mitty was saying didn't sound so ludicrous to me. Broomewode Village was plagued with suspicious deaths. It was perfectly believable that the events around the young viscount's death might have involved foul play. I thought back to scone week on the baking contest when I first met Eileen. I'd first learned about Stephen Champney when she explained about the parties at Broomewode Hall. She'd described them as elaborate, mostly for the young viscount and his friends. He was a man who'd loved life. My heart sank as I thought of the photo of my mother, Stephen Champney, the viscount, and Eileen, which I'd shown Joanna before she disappeared—along with that precious photo. How I wished I had the picture on me now to show Mitty. I was already certain that Valerie was my mother, but having Mitty call me by her name made me wonder if we looked very much alike.

Lauren and Edward appeared unbothered by Mitty's rambling. I guessed they'd been subject to it for hours. Lauren was already halfway through her sandwich, and Edward was munching on fries.

Mitty hadn't touched his food. He was frowning at the plate.

"Is there something else?" I asked Mitty, squeezing his hand, which still interlocked with mine.

"I wish I could be sure," he replied. "There were poachers about that day as well. The rifle could have belonged to one of them. But I could never figure out why Robert Champney didn't tell anyone he was out riding, too. Could he have seen his cousin go over the cliff? What did he have to hide?"

So there were poachers out too? Mitty hadn't mentioned that before. It made the evidence against Robert Champney circumstantial at best and Mitty was not the world's most reliable witness. Still, I felt a great sadness that the young viscount died like that. And now the earl had been murdered. When was the legacy of family tragedy going to stop?

I thought of Benedict, the next in line, and felt my heart shiver. Nothing must happen to him. I didn't even care if he ended up with Florence if I could keep him safe.

Mitty had called me Valerie, had said I'd remember as well. Was this why she'd left the village? Had she seen something she shouldn't? I ached for my mom. Was she scared? Bullied to leave? "Mitty," I said gently, "was Valerie there that day, too?"

He looked at me properly again, turning his gaze from the table to bore into me, his blue eyes misty and sad. "You remember that day, don't you? It's not just me."

I shook my head. What could I say? It was clear Mitty couldn't provide any straightforward answers. He still thought I was my mother. Still, we were getting somewhere, if only I could believe his memories were true. "Remind me—"

"Poppy, Eve's slammed," Philly whispered as she rushed by.

Never had I been more sorry to go back to work. I returned to the bar, moving on autopilot, my mind consumed with thoughts of Stephen Champney's terrible death and my mother and whether she'd witnessed his death. Could it be true what Joanna had said? That Valerie was in Glasgow? It seemed such an improbable place. And I'd caught a glimpse of a woman I thought might be Joanna, but then she'd vanished. If only I were a better witch, maybe I'd be a better sleuth.

As I served plates of food to the hungry funeral-goers, my own stomach rumbled. I hadn't eaten in what felt like hours, and I could also do with a strong coffee. I asked Eve if I could make an espresso for myself, and she laughed at me for being so polite. "Of course, Pops. Help yourself. You know, you're becoming more like the English every day, all worried about manners and airs and graces. Talk about assimilating."

I giggled.

"Maybe it's all that time you've been spending with the young earl," Eve said. "Funny to think of Benedict being the earl."

Her eyes were teasing and playful, but at the mention of Benedict, my heart dropped. "Hardly. I've barely seen him for obvious reasons this week, and since I ruined his father's funeral this morning, I can't imagine him wanting to spend time with me anytime soon."

I clicked the coffee maker into place and watched as the dark liquid slowly dripped from the spout into my espresso cup. "Besides, I've got competition."

"You do?" Eve looked up from where she was stacking clean pint glasses below the bar. "Surely his old girlfriend isn't back on the scene?"

"Lady Ophelia Wren? No, I heard she's back working for Doctors Without Borders. That relationship is over." I didn't think it was necessary to admit I'd actually searched online to find news of Ophelia Wren—that was a secret for me and my overly large glass of pinot noir and a boring Tuesday night at home. Anyway, the truth was much worse. "Our Lady of the Tiramisu seems to think he's fair game."

Eve spluttered with laughter. "Florence? As if. Benedict would never fall prey to a woman like that. She's so...high-maintenance."

I followed her gaze and saw that Florence had cornered Susan Bentley, who was sitting with Reg at a table in the corner. Even from my position behind the bar, I could tell that Florence was obviously on the charm offensive, and it didn't take much sleuthing to guess that she was asking for some of Susan's happy eggs for the weekend.

I looked back over at Hamish. He was watching Florence, too, and his expression was glowering.

I tipped back the coffee in one go and then went straight over to Hamish on the pretense of clearing his empties.

"Can you believe that?" he said, finally tearing his eyes away.

"Florence doesn't have exclusive access to the farm goods," I replied. "You're just as entitled to put in an order."

But Hamish shook his head. "I've more respect than to bother a woman who was friends with the earl for eggs. She's grieving."

I nodded and said I understood, but no way was I going to let Florence have an advantage over a kindhearted man like Hamish. Until today, I'd stayed on the fence about the competition, not wanting to favor either contestant. Now I was fully Team Hamish. "What if you don't have to? I've got some of Susan's happy eggs in the kitchen. I over-ordered yesterday. You can have mine."

Hamish looked delighted. He lowered his voice. "I'm glad it's Florence and not you I'm up against for the final. I wouldn't have had the heart to try to beat you. But I've no qualms about trying to take the baking crown off Florence's over-coiffed head."

He faked flicking curls over his shoulder.

I giggled. Hamish had my vote all the way.

CHAPTER 6

*a*fter the lunch rush subsided, Ruta told me to take a break and get some air. I checked on Gateau, still happily sleeping, and then left the inn, discarding the apron, which had only paid lip service—or lap service—to keeping me clean. Patches of flour and a smear of mustard marked my jeans. Not to mention the coffee stain on my white T-shirt. Oh well. It wasn't like I was in a fashion show. I needed a walk and to gather my thoughts. Unlike Florence, I didn't see the world as my stage.

The day had turned warm, the sunlight drying the last puddles from the morning's downpour. The rain had done the grounds a world of good, and the flowers gleamed like freshly polished buttons: white, purple, and blue delphiniums arranged in pretty rows, puffy heads of pink hydrangeas now coming into their own.

Without a destination in mind, I let my feet guide me. I was simply grateful to be away from people, from their specu-lation and gossip, from the snide comments I felt sure were being directed my way. The birds were chirping, and there was no one in sight. I knew the competition tent would be a hive of activity, so I steered clear. Otherwise, Broomewode was quiet, and that was exactly what I needed.

However, I hadn't left the Gerry zone yet and he caught up with me. "Don't be in such a rush, Pops. I have news."

"What kind of news?" You never knew with Gerry. He could have floated into a guest room and discovered a toupee, a smuggled-in pet snake, or that the young couple in room three were trying for a baby. All of which was interesting, but I had a lot on my mind.

"Detective news." Okay, now he had my full attention.

"The dimpled detective," and here he pushed his fingers into his cheeks to mimic dimples, "asked that nice vicar who had the key to get into the mausoleum."

"The vicar came in for a drink?" I hadn't seen him.

"Yep. And he looked like he needed it."

Oh, poor man. I felt guilty all over again for ruining the funeral.

"Oh, good point. And?"

"The vicar said they keep the key up at the hall. In the kitchen." Katie Donegal's domain, but why on earth would Katie want to kill Charles Radlier? However, she'd been charged with Robert Champney's murder, so I supposed anything was possible.

"Is it missing?"

"Don't know. But the vicar also said the lock's old and half the village lads know how to open it with a hairpin. He kept his voice down as I don't think he wanted everyone to hear, but he says he's often had to chase boys out of there. They dare each other to go down, of course." Gerry chuckled. "Sort of thing I'd have done if I lived here."

"So, basically, anyone could have found their way into the crypt?"

"Don't sound so down. I thought you'd be pleased to have the inside scoop on the investigation."

"Oh, I am, I just wish it didn't make Katie look bad. Again."

"I'm only the messenger," he reminded me. "The eyes and ears of this operation." And then he floated off toward the competition tent.

I FOLLOWED the path away from the village, trying to marshal my chaotic thoughts.

Even though I'd discovered a murder victim this morning, my mind went first to the blond woman who'd been skulking around. I was certain it was Joanna, or the woman who'd met me claiming to be Joanna, saved my life, and then disappeared. Had it really been her I'd seen skulking around the funeral? Was it just wishful thinking, me and my imagination working overtime? Or was Joanna a master at disappearing into thin air? Could it be that I'd mistaken a ghost for Joanna? We were by a graveyard, after all. But if it wasn't an apparition, why was Joanna hanging around a funeral if she didn't want to be found in Broomewode Village? That woman did not want to be found. She had been elusive from the very second we met. A sudden wave of anger hit me, and I felt the blood rise to my cheeks. I'd pinned so many hopes on this woman, and she didn't even have the decency to call me back. "How rude," I said aloud, wrinkling my nose in distaste. I wasn't used to feeling angry, and the sensation was unpleasant.

I looked to the sky, hoping for a glimpse of my hawk. The sight of him always soothed me, soaring across the blue, crying out in warning if there was danger lurking nearby. It was the most tangible sensation that my birth dad was close by, that he and the bird were inextricably linked.

But thoughts of my birth dad were painful, too. It was another mystery I'd yet to solve, another unanswered question. I had felt his presence so often here in Broomewode and communicated with his ghost during coven circles. But today I'd heard his voice, I was certain of it. I wondered if he was often near me without revealing himself, and the thought comforted me. Would I ever discover who he'd been in life?

Life and death led me to thoughts of murder. What had happened to Charles Radlier? Who had lured him to his death, and why? No doubt the police were already at work on that question. And now I was reminded of how I'd ruined Benedict's father's funeral. And then suddenly I realized where I'd walked to. Without intending to, somehow I'd walked back to the church. I was drawn towards it, propelled by some instinct I couldn't name.

As I got closer, I could see that the mausoleum was now surrounded by police tape and lots of activity. A small crowd watched the police at work, and I spotted Trim, the news reporter, off to one side, taking photos for the *Broomewode News*. It was strange to feel the buzz surrounding a crime scene, but I couldn't blame people for being curious. Finding a murdered body in a crypt during a funeral wasn't exactly your everyday occurrence. I waited to see if Charles's ghost might reappear, but I knew in my heart he'd already crossed. Fortunately, there was no sign of the other residents of the crypt, either. They must be hiding away from the noise and crowd.

Aware that people might recognize me from my outburst, I headed over to the church. There was something so soothing about its dark, cool interior. But as I climbed the stairs, the doors opened and out came Benedict.

Despite everything, my stomach flipped. He was still dressed in his funeral suit, and I wanted so desperately to put things right, but I didn't think I could find the words. Benedict came down the stairs toward me. Before he had a chance to open his mouth, I blurted out, "I'm so sorry. I know I messed up today, and I feel terrible. Truly. I hope you can forgive me."

"Forgive you? For what? You did a good thing. Imagine if Charles's body was never found? It would have been like he vanished. And whoever was responsible for putting him down there would have got away with murder."

I let out a huge sigh of relief. "You've no idea how happy I am to hear you say that. I've felt wretched all morning."

He looked strained, exhausted. "It's been a wretched day all round. I was discussing with the vicar when we might lay my father to rest."

"How's your mother coping?"

He kind of shrugged his shoulders and looked uncomfortable. "She's resting now." Which wasn't much of an answer. He glanced around the sad graveyard, his gaze drawn to the activity around his family mausoleum, then his gaze came back to rest on my face. "This is dreadful timing, but would you have dinner with me tonight? Somewhere quiet? I need to get away from all of this. If only for a few hours."

I was taken aback. And my face must have betrayed as much.

"I know it's short notice," he added.

I shook my head. "It's not that. I mean, I'd love to. But won't your mom need you?"

Benedict said, "My mother is having dinner with Florence at the hall this evening."

Maybe it was mean-spirited of me, but I was delighted he would not be joining them. In fact, he'd rather have dinner with me than Florence, which I thought showed very good taste.

Benedict's tone was even, but even I could tell he'd rather not be there—which suited me just fine. Let those two drama queens enjoy each other, and Benedict and I could be left in peace.

This day that had begun so badly seemed to be improving.

BENEDICT WENT BACK into the church, and I wandered around the graveyard, not ready to return to the inn. It was strangely peaceful here. I tried to make out the engravings on the headstones I passed, marveled at how the fashions for names changed. Merrit, Della, Elma. Corin, Dale, and Ellery. As the dates moved into the Victorian era, more recognizable names appeared. Mary, John, and James. Elizabeth and Alice. I tried to imagine all of their lives. How they struggled, loved, and laughed. All the ways these people must have been linked to one another—buying vegetables from the same stall, keeping an eye on their kids, sharing meals. Were any of them witches? Did they belong to the same coven? Had they discovered their powers slowly, one by one, like me?

As I meandered, I noticed a fresh bouquet of flowers lying beneath a tree. It was near where I'd glimpsed the blond woman earlier, the one I'd thought might be Joanna. This bouquet was much more simple than the elaborate arrangements that filled the church for the earl. A few simple white roses, pink snapdragons, and some green foliage, tied with a white ribbon. To my eye, it was prettier than the grand, formal arrangements. Perhaps someone had left it here by mistake, or maybe it had slipped from the other offerings for the funeral. I picked up the bunch, but the second my skin touched the delicate stems, a powerful sensation came over me. It was nothing like I'd experienced before, like a huge wave of nostalgia but also an ache. There was a small card attached to the bouquet, an ink outline of a single rose on its cover. I opened the card:

I love you. Forever.

Wait a minute. I'd seen this handwriting before. I dropped the bunch in shock. It was the same handwriting on the warning notes left at the inn telling me to leave Broomewode.

I bent down and examined the card again. Was my mind playing tricks on me? Could I be certain it was the same writing with only a few words? I slipped the card from the bouquet and put it into my back pocket. I set the flowers back where I'd found them. I no longer believed they were meant for Robert Champney.

I saw a figure approaching and then Trim's face appeared,

his enormous Canon digital camera hung round his neck. Rather than his usual uniform of white shirt and jeans, he was dressed in a dark, slightly crumpled suit. He'd obviously been hanging around the police investigators. Trim wasn't one to miss a scoop—and Charles Radlier's murder had all the hallmarks of an epic news report.

We greeted each other, and I immediately asked if he'd discovered anything useful.

He glanced at his watch. "I've got to get back and write my story, but I can give you a couple of highlights."

"Great."

"No official COD yet." Seeing my puzzled expression, he said, "That's cause of death, not cash on delivery." He cast an annoyed glance behind him. "Though cash might well have been behind his murder. I got precious little out of the officials, but the locals who knew him have more to say. He had money problems and an expensive, nasty divorce."

I already knew the cause of death, but the rest of what Trim had to say did interest me, and confirmed some of the rumors.

"So he was a single man."

He nodded, significantly. "Single and I heard he spent the entire week comforting Evelyn Champney in her bereavement." He shook his head. "If you hadn't heard something, he'd never have been found."

I didn't want him to ask me about that, so I asked if Charles Radlier had had a rival for Evelyn Champney's affections.

Trim nodded. "That's what I like about you, Poppy. Once you set your mind to do something, you just paddle your own canoe until you get there. You'd make an excellent reporter if you fancy a career change."

I laughed, ignoring the suggestion of becoming a news reporter. I'd already had enough career changes. "Paddle your own canoe?" I said. "I like that expression."

"An old idiom." Trim chuckled. "But yes. I believe the earl's widow would only have remained single by choice. Anyway, I must dash. Another great story. It's almost as big as the earl's death itself." He looked very pleased with himself. "I'm hoping to make a move to a bigger paper, and these huge stories are great for my career." He suddenly went serious. "Though terrible for Broomewode, of course."

I watched him go and then, hoping Mavis wouldn't be quite as deadline-crazed, decided to follow. Mavis was Joanna's mother, and if anyone would know if her daughter had been at this morning's funeral, it ought to be her. Come to think of it, I couldn't remember seeing Mavis there, but it had been a bit of a stressful time.

Continuing my walk, I made my way to the office of the *Broomewode News*.

By now I recognized the woman who manned the newspaper's reception desk. She was having an argument with someone on the phone about paying for their advertising. She raised her carefully penciled eyebrows at me, and I mimed I was here to see Mavis. Taking the slight dip of her head as acquiescence, I climbed the stairs to Mavis's office and knocked on the door.

"Come in," she called out. I opened the door, and the familiar smell of dust and aging newspaper hit me. There was Mavis, sitting at her old schoolteacher's desk, surrounded by papers.

Mavis looked up, and her deep-set brown eyes were full of surprise at seeing me. Perhaps she'd witnessed my funeral-destroying behavior this morning. A pair of glasses were hanging on a gold chain around her neck, and she'd clearly dressed for the earlier weather in a light sweater. "Oh hello, Poppy," she said. "Do come in."

I apologized for turning up unannounced and took a seat opposite her desk. "I know you must be very busy with this morning's events, gathering info and speaking to witnesses, but I wondered if I could just borrow a minute of your time."

"Of course, dear," Mavis replied, although she was still typing away at the computer. Her eyes traveled briefly back to the screen and then she said, "And send," with a flourish. She turned her attention back to me. "Honestly, I can't understand why everyone emails these days. My inbox is never cleared." She shuffled a few papers and then said, "Now, tell me what I can help you with today. Surely you've spoken with my daughter already?"

"That's the thing—I'm having trouble reaching Joanna. She was picking up her cell, and now the number has gone out of service."

Mavis looked bemused. "Are you sure you've been ringing the right phone? That's not like her. My Joanna's always prompt at returning calls and emails." She glanced at a photo behind her desk. I followed her gaze. The photo was recent, of Mavis with gray hair and her warm, wide smile. Her arm was around a woman with red hair.

Red hair. Eve had said Joanna used to have red hair.

Tingles shot down my neck. "Is that you and Joanna?" I asked, already knowing the answer.

"Of course. That was taken at the village fete a couple of years ago."

My suspicion was confirmed. The woman in the photo was not the "Joanna" who had met me at The Hourglass café.

Which begged the obvious question: Who had pretended to be Joanna?

And why?

CHAPTER 7

*T*wandered back to the inn in shock, my feet moving seemingly of their own accord. So much had happened today, I didn't know how to process it all. I kept my head down as I walked through the village streets, paranoid that everyone was talking about me. All I wanted was to get back in bed and curl up with Gateau. My heart was hurting. So many people were not what they seemed. I was disappointed in Florence and her behavior, "Joanna" and all her lies. Nothing and no one was straightforward around here, and I'd had enough of it all.

Yet as I got closer to the inn, I began to calm down. By now I knew that instant shift in feeling could only come from one of my coven sisters, my elder most likely. I stopped in my tracks and looked around. Sure enough, Elspeth Peach emerged from the right-hand path, which converged onto mine. She lifted a hand in greeting, and I took deep breaths, so grateful for the warmth Elspeth emanated. And then I saw what was in her other hand. "Gateau!" I cried. Elspeth set my feline familiar down, and she scampered over to me.

"I found her gnawing at the hydrangea bush, the naughty puss," Elspeth said, laughing. She was still wearing funeral attire—simple black trouser suit and string of pearls at her neck—but she'd let down her white hair, and now it hung neatly by her shoulders.

I cradled Gateau to my chest and immediately felt better.

"That's more like it, Poppy," Elspeth said, half laughing. "You should have seen the scowl on your face whilst you were walking. I sensed your distress miles away."

She linked her arm through mine and steered me off the path and across the grass. "Witches always feel better when they're connected to the earth—even water witches like you, Poppy. In fact, why don't we visit the lake?"

I'd been wanting to catch up with Elspeth properly for so long that I agreed immediately, no matter that it was only a stone's throw from Broomewode Hall and therefore in the countess's domain. I hoped I wouldn't have to face the woman whose husband's funeral I'd so spectacularly ruined. I let Elspeth lead the way and answered honestly as she questioned me about my troubles.

Without pausing for breath, I explained all about Joanna and then my embarrassment at insisting I could hear something in the crypt, leading to the discovery of Charles Radlier's body. I was tired of the deception that seemed rife in Broomewode, but most of all I was tired of being disappointed in myself. "I'm infuriated, really," I said, "infuriated that I'm not a better witch."

"A better witch?" Elspeth asked, genuinely surprised. "Tell me, what do you think being a better witch involves?"

"Understanding my powers, being able to control them and use them properly for good. I just feel like...I'm assaulted by my powers. They seem impossible to wrangle. Everything new that's happened to me since I arrived in Broomewode has appeared out of nowhere, and I don't know how to control it. Moving things by sight, visions in water, and now it seems I'm more connected to the ghost world than I'd thought. How did I hear that poor ghost banging and cursing through all those layers of stone and marble?"

Elspeth smiled gently and encouraged me to slow down.

"Remember how I told you that Broomewode Village is built on an energy vortex, how it draws our kind towards it?"

I nodded. How could I forget? It was like, never mind the baking competition; you're being messed with by magical forces you can't see. It had been a lot for a girl to take in.

"What's happening to you," Elspeth continued, "is that everything is arriving all at once. You're like a magnet, attracting forms of magic that were always within grasp but are now coming to you quickly as you become more receptive. More open to your powers."

Great, so now I was a giant magnet? Would paper clips start flying across rooms and attach themselves to me? I didn't know whether to laugh or cry.

"It's very exciting," Elspeth insisted. Which was one way to look at it.

Though not mine.

We arrived at the lake, which was as lovely as ever in the afternoon sun. The swans were serene and elegant as they floated past water lilies and cattails. A few green-headed mallards ducked for food, their fluffy behinds sticking out of the water. We stood still, looking into the water—the site of my first-ever vision of Valerie, pregnant and scared.

I closed my eyes, trying to stay calm. But the sight of the

lake was only fueling my frustration. I felt as clueless as I had eight weeks ago.

"The full spectrum of your powers is already present within you. The energy vortex brings some of them to the surface, but the others you need to access yourself." Elspeth paused and then smiled knowingly. "Which is why I thought you'd like some help."

As if from nowhere, Susan and Eve appeared on the horizon. They were each carrying a basket. Gateau mewed and rolled happily on the bank of the lake.

"What's going on?" I asked. "Shouldn't Eve be at the pub? Susan must be needed back at the farm, too?"

"Don't worry," Elspeth said. "Nothing is more important to a witch than another witch in need."

Susan and Eve joined us and stood by my side. They set their baskets down.

"Don't look so worried, Pops. We're here to help."

"It's broad daylight!" I exclaimed. "Surely we can't have a magic circle now? Don't we need the light of the moon and to be, well, inconspicuous?"

Susan chuckled. "It's not a circle. But we are here to show you where your powers come from." She turned her gaze to the lake and then began to unpack candles from her basket. Elspeth promptly lit them with a flick of her hands.

"You're a water witch, Poppy," Elspeth said quietly. "It's your medium. Now you need to learn to trust your instincts and let the water guide you. It's the source of your powers. You need to concentrate and ask the water for answers. It will help you understand how to control your special gifts. They're sacred and ancient."

Despite myself, I could feel tears forming in my eyes. More water.

Elspeth turned to face the lake, and the four of us stood in a semicircle and joined hands. Gateau crawled onto my feet and nestled herself there snugly like a pair of comfy slippers.

Elspeth began to murmur a chant under her breath. The words were still unintelligible to me, so I let them wash over my mind and fixed my gaze on the surface of the water. Birdsong grew in volume, chirping and tweeting as if joining in our ritual. The water of the lake was still. Too still. I didn't know where to focus my attention. On the surface? The reeds and plant life that ringed the edges? The swans were a distraction, swimming into my field of vision. But I felt Eve's hand grip mine tighter, and the electric charge between us strengthened, even though we hadn't formed a complete circle.

I closed my eyes, listened to the breeze running through the branches. All of a sudden the scent of pine resin filled my nostrils. Then the sound of creaking pine cones. Swishing needles. But there were no pine trees in Broomewode, were there?

My eyes snapped open.

The lake was swirling, almost imperceptibly, but the movement was there. I hadn't noticed that Eve and Susan had joined in Elspeth's chant. I closed my eyes again. The water was trying to tell me something, to take me to another place. I could feel it with every fiber of my body. I took deep breaths in and out, allowed myself to feel the breeze that was gathering, to inhale the scent of the pine trees, and then opened my eyes again.

I gasped. On the surface of the water was a mirage of woodland. It both was and wasn't the woods behind Broomewode Hall where Gina and I almost met our end in my very first week on the baking show. I leaned forward. Gateau was standing now, glued to my side. The water was growing darker in color like it was reflecting a twilight sky—soft purples and patches of pinks, mysterious and enchanting like the feeling of being half awake and half still in a dream. The surface was covered now with trees, some in the foreground, some dim silhouettes, but the presence of pine trees was clear. Unmistakable. A breeze made the pines shiver, and needles fell to the earth. Someone was in the woods—I could feel them. The light in the scene shifted again, and now it was dark, pitch dark, until suddenly a crack of silver moonlight appeared and cast a piercing white beam between the trees. The season was autumn. The branches were bare, curling out and reaching towards each other like some kind of spiral staircase heading for the moon. Fallen leaves covered the woodland floor, reds and rusts and gold. Dry and brown and furling into themselves. A carpet on the earth. There was rustling now, the sound of cautious footsteps. Two sets. No, wait. Was it three?

"Who's there?" I found myself calling out.

There was no answer.

I tried again.

"Who's there?"

Nothing.

Suddenly an electric jolt caused me to shake. It was more than the force of my coven sisters put together. I was trembling, but Eve, Susan, and Elspeth did not stop their chant. Someone was nearby, both in the lake's mirage and in the grounds around us. I was on high alert.

As I continued to tremble from the current, the women's chant grew louder. I was afraid someone would hear us, but it occurred to me that Elspeth might have put a magic shield around us. There was so much I didn't know. "Give me answers," I demanded of the water. "What are you trying to tell me?"

The lake's surface rippled again, and then silhouettes became clear. It was Valerie, my mother. And there was my father. They were younger than they'd ever appeared to me before, holding hands, walking and laughing and so palpably in love, my heart softened. This was where I came from—a place of so much affection. My mom and dad snuggled into each other, two peas in a pod, arms encircling waists. My eyes were still wet, and I let the tears spill over and rush down my cheeks.

But what was that behind them?

The third silhouette. I squinted. But the image wasn't clear. It was another person, that much was for sure, but their face was cast in darkness. There was danger there. Someone was following them with evil intent. I felt the sharp hitch of jealousy so clearly. I wanted to call out and warn them, but the words were stuck in my throat.

"Danger!" I finally cried. "Get out! It's not safe here. You've got to leave!"

And with those words, the image disappeared. The water stilled. The swans returned. Autumn shifted back to summer. Darkness turned to light.

I was still shaking, filled with frustration. Why couldn't they hear me?

And then I realized which words had come so easily to me. *Get out. It's not safe here. You've got to leave.* The same words that my dad's ghost and my mom's mirage had said to me. The same words of warning Joanna had spoken. The same words written on the anonymous note.

"You're safe, my dear," Elspeth said softly. But was I?

"You were somewhere else entirely," Susan said.

"What did you see?" Eve asked.

I looked at the three of them in surprise. "You didn't see it as well?"

They shook their heads. "See what?" Elspeth asked gently.

"The lake. It became woodland. The woods behind Broomewode Hall. My birth mom and dad were there. They were young; it was before I was born. And there was someone else. The smell of pine trees was so overpowering. The trees were important, but I couldn't figure out why. They were in danger. The third person was someone bad. They couldn't hear me warn them..."

My coven sisters stared at me kindly. "It's okay," Elspeth said. "You were being shown the past, not the present. Whatever happened has already been and gone."

"But they were here. I'm sure of it. It wasn't London. My mother and father were here in Broomewode. Why have so many people lied to me?" A bad feeling had lodged itself inside me, and I couldn't shake it.

"Poppy," Eve said.

There was something in her tone that made me snap out of my haze.

"Look," she said, pointing across the water.

It was a pine cone. And it was skimming the surface of the water, floating over to us as if riding the air.

I stared at it, and then the cone picked up pace. It came

rushing towards me, lifting up from the water and straight into my open hand. My jaw dropped open. I hadn't even realized I was holding out my hand. But there it was.

"You did that!" Susan cried gleefully. "You brought the pine cone to you all the way from the woods, across the grounds, over the water, and into your hand."

"I did?" I replied, genuinely confused.

Elspeth and Eve were nodding.

"The source of your power is the water," Elspeth said, "and now you're becoming strong enough to get it to do your bidding. I think that instead of the visions revealing themselves to you, you are, in fact, summoning them. You're more in control than you know, Poppy. Your magic is growing. *You* are growing."

CHAPTER 8

*G*ateau and I walked back to the inn alone. I told the others I needed some time to process what had happened at the lake. They understood, of course, and sent me away with Susan's basket, which was full of happy eggs for Hamish. Susan really did think of everything. I hugged them all, pressing them to me, whispering how grateful I was for the guidance.

I was in a daze, confused and upset by the scene I'd witnessed, yet also reminded of the love between my birth parents. The warnings I'd received over the weeks now took on a new weight. Why had the exact same words come out of my mouth? It hadn't been a conscious decision; it was more like they were buried in my psyche, waiting to release themselves. Could that just be the result of hearing and reading them so many times? Or was it something deeper?

Even Gateau didn't seem her usual self. Her gait was slow, not perky, and she'd been suspiciously meow-less since the lake. No number of strokes subdued her disquiet. I was worried. But I couldn't let it fester. Tonight, I was finally getting to have dinner with Benedict, and I was determined to show up at my best and most charming. After all, it wasn't like I could explain why I was distracted.

As we approached the inn, Gateau scampered off. I guessed she needed some alone time. As my familiar, she'd been part of that extraordinary scene too. Who knew what that mischievous cat got up to when I wasn't around, but she'd earned a break.

Inside, the pub was still buzzing. Eve had the evening off after the busy lunch rush, and Belinda, the kitchen girl from Broomewode Hall and fellow junior witch, was helping out Philly for the dinner service. I waved at Belinda, and she grinned back, dark eyes sparkling and a broad smile stretching across her freckled face.

I was surprised to see that many of the Londoners who'd made the trip up for the earl's funeral hadn't moved since lunch. Some were playing cards, others deep into another bottle of wine. The whole scene was very convivial—the only clue something dreadful had happened was that most people were still in their black funeral outfits. It got me thinking about the earl's popularity again. I remembered how pompous and embarrassing Robert Champney had been when he'd brought his family in here for dinner a few weeks ago. He had tried to be "matey" with the locals, but it was obvious that he really didn't fit in. Who were Robert's real friends? Did he have any beyond Susan Bentley? Even his hunting buddies, Charles Radlier and Harrison Zucker, had put the moves on his wife the minute he was off the scene.

I scanned the room and saw that for the first time ever, the remaining bakers weren't sitting together for dinner. Florence and her dashing producer were at the bar drinking glasses of champagne. Hamish was sitting with Edward and Lauren. Although both Hamish and Florence looked perfectly content to be apart, I was struck by the sadness of it. We'd begun this journey as a supportive group, helping each other, buoying one another up when the going got tough. As the weeks went on and the group became smaller, we became friends. Or at least I thought we had. Now there wasn't even a semblance of cordiality between the remaining two contestants.

I was going to deliver Hamish's happy eggs and then slip upstairs and get ready for my date, but Florence spotted me and waved me over. Oh, dear. I didn't want to listen to her gloat again about the la-di-da evening she had planned with 'Evelyn.' That woman hated my guts, and I was about to go on a date with her son. Talk about feeling unwelcome in the family.

Florence was looking extraordinarily glamorous. Still in black, she'd changed into a relaxed linen suit, complete with two strands of pearls around her throat and matching drop earrings—an ensemble more Elspeth Peach than Florence Cinelli. Maybe she was modeling herself on the famous baking judge, preparing for her new career. It seemed manipulative even for Florence. Her hair was down and her face perfectly painted, makeup demure but crafted to enhance her pretty features. It was hard not to admire her skill in the makeup department. No, that wasn't fair. She had incredible skill in the kitchen, as well. As much as I wanted Hamish to win, I knew she was the stronger competitor going in.

"Where did you get to, Pops?" Florence cooed.

Well, my coven sisters and I gathered at the lake, where I had a vision of my birth parents walking in the woods. Thanks for asking.

I shrugged. "Oh, you know, out for some air."

Florence offered me a glass of champagne, but I declined.

"Looks like you're already celebrating," I said. "It's not like you to drink before filming."

Florence raised a brow. "Champagne doesn't count, darling. I expect that's what the Champneys will serve this evening at dinner."

Well, it didn't take long for her to drop that little bit of info again.

"Even though it's going to be a cozy dinner—just the family," she added, her eyes slanting to see how I took the news.

I smiled politely. Let Florence think that Benedict would be joining them. Hopefully, we'd be far away from Broomewode Village and all the drama that went with it by the time she realized he wouldn't be joining them.

Florence was too busy posing to notice that I was carrying Susan's basket, so I wished her a pleasant evening and went to the table where Hamish sat looking glum.

"How are you holding up?" I asked as I arrived at the table and slipped into the spare chair. I couldn't imagine the pressure he was under right now.

"I'm a mess of nerves, to be honest."

I patted his hand. "Maybe this will help." I lifted the muslin teacloth that protected Susan's bounty.

Hamish's eyes glowed. "Thank you," he said, obviously relieved Florence wouldn't be the only one with happy eggs.

I told Hamish he was more than welcome. I was tempted to add some extra magic to the eggs but knew it would break the sacred code of not using magic for our own gain. Although technically it would be Hamish's gain, but still, Elspeth's warning rang in my ears.

I asked Hamish about his plan for tonight, and he told me he was going to grab a bite to eat and then work all evening, going over his final designs for the showstopper.

His evening was a stark contrast to Florence's lavish dinner over at the grand hall. Was she confident or foolhardy? It was hard to tell. But I knew if the shoe was on the other foot, I'd make the same choices as Hamish. I asked him about his showstopper. "As long as you don't think it'll jinx it," I added quickly. I knew that all bakers had their superstitions, and last week none of the contestants wanted to talk about their bakes.

But Hamish was happy to talk it through. The final week was Banquet Week. "We're supposed to approach each task as if it were to be served at a banquet. A banquet!" Hamish looked plain confused. I didn't imagine he spent a lot of his time catering banquets.

"Oh," I murmured. No wonder Florence was feeling so confident—she was born to banquet. Hamish was more farm than formal.

"What's the showstopper?" I asked.

"We have to make six different entremets cakes."

"Oh, man."

"You're telling me. I didn't even know what an entremet was before last week. And then I find out that it has *multiple* components assembled in layers. Poppy, when this is over, I may never bake a layer again."

I smiled because I understood so well the stress he was under.

"One of them is a mousse, enrobed with a glaze and then topped with fine decorations. You know how I am with the finishing touches." He let out a giant sigh.

I reassured Hamish that his presentation skills had come on in leaps and bounds over the last few weeks. "Besides, entremets can come in all different colors, shapes, and sizes and showcase a variety of flavor combinations and textures. You can spin this to your advantage."

"Exactly. Crunchy, creamy, mousse-y, bubbly, cakey—you name it, I've got to bake it. And we have to make six. They're supposed to look stunning, like edible art, revealing perfect layers when you slice into them. There are just so many steps, Pops. I don't know how to keep on top of it all. The main problem is the setting time needed between layers. I'm going to have to work lightning-fast and make the chill blaster my new best friend. And you know how hard that is when the nerves kick in."

I could feel my eyes widening. "Wait—six of them? Surely not full-size?"

Hamish widened his eyes so that the whites popped. "Not full-size, but not miniature, either. I'm not sure that's a bonus. I've got fingers and thumbs like Cumberland sausages—delicate work is not for me. And they all have to have different flavors. And look like they belong on a plate. Och, it's going to be brutal."

Poor Hamish. Hadn't he just heard me say his presentation skills had improved? I wasn't lying. He had improved so much since we all began together. He kept his head under pressure, possibly a skill he'd learned as a police officer. I figured I'd just keep repeating my reassurances. "Besides," I added, "it's not all about how things look." I turned in my chair and angled my head to where Florence was still quaffing champagne at the bar. "You have to have substance, too."

Hamish's eyes twinkled mischievously, and I was relieved I'd managed to distract him from his woe. "I mean, honestly, what's that lassie's game? Off gallivanting at the hall the night before filming?"

"I think she believes her own hype," I said quietly. "But..." I needed to share my secret, and who better to trust than Hamish? "Oh, this is mean. But her bubble is about to burst."

Hamish leaned closer. I was positive that at this moment he wasn't worrying about tomorrow. "Do tell."

"She's expecting to dine with the dowager countess and the new earl tonight at the hall." I leaned closer, "Or Evelyn and Ben, as she likes to call them."

Hamish might not be a detective, but he had the skills. I didn't need to tell him more. His eyes crinkled in a smile. "But someone key will be missing."

I nodded, a small smile playing around my lips. "I have a date with Benedict tonight." I still couldn't believe it.

"Good for you, Poppy. You deserve something lovely to happen to you."

I glowed. "Speaking of which, it's time to get ready."

I wished Hamish a fruitful night of study and said good-bye. Lauren and Edward were sitting together nearby, sharing a plate of fries. They looked so cozy and comfortable in each other's company. Would Benedict and I be that natural together?

I CLIMBED THE STAIRS, mentally preparing my outfit for dinner. Thank goodness I'd packed that summer dress for Sunday's filming. How should I wear my hair? Up or down? And my makeup, for that matter. I'd become so used to my best friend, Gina, who did hair and makeup for *The Great British Baking Contest,* doing my glam. It was going to be hard to replicate her talent for making me look more presentable. I'd texted her, of course, to see if she could help me out for the big date, and she'd phoned me immediately, excited as anything. But her tone changed when I told her who the date was with. This was the girl who'd been begging me to let some romance into my life for too long to mention. But when I said Benedict's name, there was just silence on the other end of the line. I'd asked her what was wrong, my heart sinking. But she'd just laughed brightly and said nothing was wrong—she was just surprised.

I didn't think he was your type, she said. To be honest, neither did I. But then the heart wants what the heart wants. Gina had apologized. *Imagine you in that grand hall,* she said. *I could channel Grace Kelly and set your hair in waves.* I'd explained that we'd be going as far away from Broomewode as possible, and Gina had laughed and said it was probably wise. She would have loved to help but was stuck on another makeup job until nine p.m. *Do call me afterwards,* she'd insisted as we hung up. *I want to know how it goes. Gory detail by gory detail.*

I put my key into the door, but before I used my magic to turn it without touching, I already knew Gerry was in my room. Was it really that my witch instincts were getting stronger, or was Gerry just predictable?

I laughed to myself as I focused on making the key turn

by magic. Gerry was floating by the wardrobe when I walked in.

"There you are," he said with all the exaggerated annoyance of a parent waiting for their teenager to get home.

I closed the door. "Well, this *is* my room, if you hadn't noticed."

"I like to think of the entire inn as my domain," Gerry informed me. "I mean, it's the only one I've got. Besides, don't get uppity with me—I've been a very good spy while you've been off doing whatever it is you do when you go AWOL."

Now Gerry had my attention. "What have you heard? Do you have a lead on Charles Radlier's murder?"

"Yes, but that's not the juiciest thing."

I urged him to go on.

Gerry turned a somersault in the air. "As you may have noticed, our dear Florence is on one big ego trip."

"I thought you were going to tell me something I didn't know," I said, heading for the wardrobe.

"Hold your horses. I heard her talking to her producer fellow, and it's clear that Florence will stop at nothing to win. She was going on and on about being the next Elspeth Peach, only younger and prettier."

My skin prickled at the insult. "Oh, how dare she."

"Right? I've been practicing moving things around so I can knock her ingredients over in the tent tomorrow. Imagine," he swept his arms out theatrically, "flour everywhere. On the floor, down her dress, in her hair."

I appreciated Gerry's feelings but begged him not to interfere. "I want Hamish to win, too, but it should be fair. We can't get involved, no matter how tempting it might be to see Florence dunked in flour."

Gerry frowned and pouted like a toddler whose toys had been taken away. "It's not like Florence plays fair. Look at the way she's going after your man."

I tutted. "Benedict is his own man."

"If only I could float up to the hall and eavesdrop, but no matter how hard I try, I can't go that far."

More was the pity. I wouldn't mind hearing what went on behind the scenes at Broomewode Hall, although I suspected it might make my blood curdle.

I thought it best to change the subject. "Have you over-heard anything of use in the pub?"

"Mrs. Simmons is feeling ever so much better now her gallbladder's out."

I giggled. "You know I don't mean that kind of thing." I waved Gerry away from the wardrobe and unhooked my dress for this evening, laying it carefully out on the bed.

Gerry poked out his tongue and waggled his ears. "I did hear more about Katie Donegal and her feud with the butcher."

He definitely had my attention, now. "You did?"

"Yes, Belinda from Broomewode Hall was talking to someone from the dairy farm. Apparently, Derek admitted to the farmer that Katie was always sending him rude notes. He's planning to tell the police."

"That's what Katie said all along, that those notes found on the earl's desk were meant for the butcher. But will anyone believe that?"

"Or will it seem like she was a vicious character who sent terrible notes to people?" He made a back-and-forth motion with his hand. "Could go either way."

That was not what Katie needed. She was only just out on bail.

"I don't like the woman, mind, but I don't want to see an older lady locked up in jail for murder," Gerry continued. "Especially if you're so convinced the earl's death has nothing to do with her."

"Why don't you like Katie?" I was surprised at Gerry's opinion.

"Don't know. There's something dodgy with her always trying to keep you from Mitty. I don't think she's been honest with you from the start."

I tended to agree, but that didn't make her a murderer. Just not a very reliable friend.

What could I do? It's not like I could defend Katie on the note front—she did write rude letters to the butcher. But that didn't make her a murderer. If it was possible to prove the notes found on the earl's desk were intended for Derek, that ought to help Katie's case.

"That's not all," Gerry said, positively gloating now. "I also heard two posho Londoners talking. They were at the hunt last week and one was telling the other about the earl's financial advisor, Harrison Zucker, and Charles Radlier having a row last week. It was about money."

"That seems to be a running theme with Charles. Was he really in that much debt? Or is it idle gossip?"

Gerry shrugged and admitted it was sometimes hard to know the difference. However, what he'd gleaned was that Robert Champney had shared his suspicions that Charles was pinching money from the hunting fund.

I raised my eyebrows. "I can't imagine the earl took that lightly."

"Nope. But of course he wouldn't dirty his own hands, accusing his Master of the Hunt of pinching the dosh. Instead, he sent Harrison to talk to Charles, and they had a big old barney. Even more interesting, after the earl died, Zucker told Charles to keep clear of the countess."

"Interesting. Maybe it means they both had their eye on the widowed Lady Frome, though I can't see what the appeal is myself. That woman is cold as ice."

"Her poor deceased husband isn't half as cold as she is." Gerry agreed. "Perhaps her money will keep them warm."

"When did the fight between Charles and Harrison take place?"

Gerry said he couldn't be sure, but it seemed very recent. "Maybe even yesterday morning. Seems both men came to Broomewode Hall to comfort the countess. Maybe Harrison got rid of his competition," Gerry said. "He looks the type to know where the bodies are buried."

I shuddered at his choice of phrase, as I'd been the one who discovered where that particular body was buried. With some pretty uncomfortable results.

CHAPTER 9

I'd banished Gerry while I got ready for my date. My phone buzzed as I was putting the final touches to my makeup. It was Benedict—he was five minutes away and wanted me to meet him in the car park.

Good thinking, I texted back, glad I'd be able to slip away from the inn unnoticed. *See you soon.*

I deliberated for a moment and then sent another message with just an X.

My heart flipped when he replied in kind. I stared at the glowing X and finally allowed myself to become excited about the evening ahead. I turned and faced the mirror. I had to admit the dress looked great on me, and even without Gina's help, I'd done a respectable job with my makeup and hair. *No more sleuthing, no more witching around,* I said firmly to my reflection. *You're looking far too good to mess this one up.*

I grinned at myself. The dress was so pretty. It was a vintage shop find, and the cut was classic and uniformly flattering—or at least that's what Gina had told me. I just liked its simplicity and how it made me feel when I slipped the straps over my shoulders. I'd paired it with cotton espadrilles and a light blue shawl that matched the trim. Eve's silver amulet stayed on my wrist, but I removed Elspeth's necklace, as it didn't work with the line of the dress. Instead, I slipped the protective jewelry into my clutch bag so it would stay by my side and I could have the full strength of the Elspeth protective spell. You just never knew what was round the corner these days. I'd kept my makeup light, just a bit of mascara, pink cream blush, and berry lipstick, and used the inn's hairdryer to blow-dry my hair straight. It fell in a soft sheet down past my shoulders.

After Gerry had left, Gateau resurfaced, and now I kissed her little face goodbye. She appeared to grimace, embarrassed by the pet-mom love, but I didn't care—I was floating on nothing but good vibes, and not even a grouchy familiar was going to burst that bubble. "Wish me luck," I whispered. She meowed pretty half-heartedly, but I'd take it.

I sneaked down the stairs, slipped through the hallway and out the back door, which led to the car park. At seven p.m. it was still light out, but the sky was taking on that lovely pink quality that would deepen to purple as true dusk arrived. I let my shawl slip from my shoulders and prayed that I hadn't overdone it with my outfit. For all I knew, we were going for fish and chips at a pub. Though somehow I doubted it.

The car park was bursting at the seams, and I scanned the rows of shiny cars before realizing I didn't even know what vehicle Benedict drove. There was so much I didn't know about this man. Yet the thought of him sent blood rushing to my cheeks. I felt a deep connection to him, an intimacy that felt entirely natural. Tonight was a chance to find out if the real Benedict Champney was the man I thought he was. Every part of me hoped my instincts wouldn't let me down.

Of course, the future was so complicated, I couldn't think beyond tonight. As his mother had made very clear to me, he was a huge matrimonial catch now that he was the Earl of Frome. And who was I? A witch, nothing complicated there! And a woman who had wonderful parents but something strange about her birth parents. Would I ever find out where I'd come from?

A sharp honk broke me from my reverie, and I followed the noise until I saw a burgundy classic car. Benedict was smiling and waving, and I walked towards him slowly, taking in the full glory of the car. I was no auto aficionado, but I could tell straightaway it was a Bentley. Benedict got out and came to open the door for me. He was wearing a dark blue suit and white shirt, brown hair brushed away from his face, and the effect was so handsome that I found myself acting goofy. "Now don't you look nice when you make an effort," I joked.

"I could say the same, but instead I'll tell you that you look lovely this evening." He leaned over and kissed the side of my mouth softly before opening the passenger door.

Glowing from his touch, I slipped into the soft biscuit-colored leather seats. "This is some ride," I said as Benedict took his side. The dashboard looked to be carved from maple, the wood tones rippling and polished to a high shine.

"Nineteen fifty-eight Bentley S-Type Continental Flying Spur. Normally I bomb around in the old Land Rover, but for an occasion such as this, I thought my father's Bentley was more the ticket."

I listened for a note of sorrow in his voice at the mention of his dad, but it stayed steady.

"Besides, we'll be selling it off soon, and it's the most marvelous thing to drive."

"You're going to sell it?" Somehow it seemed to suit him better than I could have imagined.

He pulled a face. "Death duties."

"Right." I didn't understand much about how those worked, but it seemed that old family fortunes got whittled away after every death.

He put the car into drive, and soon we were leaving Broomewode. It occurred to me I still didn't know where we were going. Benedict laughed when I asked him and said as far away as was possible in an evening, and when I was still nonplussed, he told me we were heading into Bath.

I was pleased and told him so. "I love the city," I said. "I love how it's managed to hold on to its old Roman roots. All the old architecture is so well-preserved. And the streets are clean and tidy. Like a chocolate box image. Except it's lively, too. So many nice shops and restaurants and green spaces even though it's a bustling city."

"They should hire you at the tourism board."

I laughed. "No more jobs for me." I was so busy between working at the inn and doing my graphic design.

I was surprised at how comfortable I felt with Benedict as he confidently zipped through the country lanes and onto the A-road that would take us into the city. He was relaxed and charming, telling me about the restaurant he'd chosen.

"We've been going there since I was a child," he said. "It's very classic, quiet, and the staff are lovely. But it's the food which stands out. I have to admit, given your talent as a pastry chef, I was a little intimidated to choose somewhere for us to go."

I laughed. "You're joking, right?" Benedict was probably born eating caviar.

"Not at all. You have an amazing palate, and I didn't want to disappoint you."

I was touched and laid a hand on his knee. "I'm sure it's going to be perfect."

I wound down the window and let the evening breeze rush into the car, taking deep lungfuls of the country air.

Before long, Benedict was pulling into The Circus, a historic ring of huge Georgian townhouses that formed three horseshoe shapes, which linked together to make a grand ring. He turned into a side lane, where a small but elegant-looking restaurant was tucked beneath a dark green awning.

"Here," he said, turning off the engine and smiling. "Let me get your door."

I was about to insist that I could open my own door perfectly well but stopped myself in time. Benedict was all about the old-fashioned chivalry, and who was I to complain? It was nice to be treated like a lady.

Benedict also opened the restaurant door, and we were greeted warmly by a gray-haired maître d' dressed in an impeccable suit.

"Lord Frome, what a pleasure to have you dine with us this evening."

Benedict frowned a little but shook the maître d's hand. "Francois," he said, "you must call me Benedict. Why, you've known me since I was this high." He tapped his knees, and the maître d' laughed. "And this is Poppy."

Francois shook my hand and complimented my dress. I

blushed, feeling like a movie star. Delicious food smells wafted through the air, and I realized I was ravenous.

"Come then, Benedict, your usual table is waiting."

I felt proud as we walked through the restaurant. The interiors were beautiful: abstract paintings with vivid splashes of color hung from muted olive walls, the tables beneath laid with fine silverware and cut crystal glasses sitting atop crisp white linen tablecloths. Candles flickered, and the low lighting shone from carefully placed floor lamps in between tables. The result was elegant but inviting, too. Like dining inside some fancy artist's London townhouse. It was buzzing with conversation and laughter, and I was relieved to be somewhere I was a stranger and no one recognized me. We arrived at a table for two in a quiet alcove.

"Enjoy your meal," Francois said, pulling out my chair.

"Thank you, Francois," said Benedict, seating himself.

Francois bowed his head a little and said our waiter would be right over.

I looked at my date. "You're going to have to get used to being the earl and addressed accordingly. Why do you fight it?"

Benedict sighed. "I know you're right, but somehow I never imagined I'd be the earl. It doesn't feel like me, somehow. It was my father's obsession and my mother's, not mine."

I nodded, but I knew it was grief talking. He was still in shock and it would take time for him to comfortably step into his father's shoes. It wasn't up to me to press the matter. I could already tell Benedict was going to be a fabulous earl and totally different from his father. He was kind and friendly, genuine with everyone he met. I could tell the people of Broomewode liked him for himself, where his father had been tolerated.

He ordered us two champagne cocktails, and I watched with delight as the waiter set down the sparkling coupe glasses, a fizzing angostura-soaked sugar cube nestled at the bottom. It was a classic drink that went well with the classic car and Benedict's classic sensibility.

We pored over the menu together, Benedict talking me through the restaurant's specialties. According to him, there were several dishes I simply had to try, and we ended up ordering far too much food: pork rillettes, dressed crab, and chicken fried in pine-infused breadcrumbs to start; beef bourguignon for me and grilled sole with lemon caper butter for Benedict, with sides of crushed new potatoes and char-grilled purple sprouting broccoli. I sat back, anticipating a fantastic meal.

I took a sip of my cocktail, and I realized I felt the most relaxed and comfortable I'd been in weeks. Strange, as the day had been so tumultuous. I told Benedict as much, and he nodded, taking both my hands in his.

"I know what you mean. When I'm with you, Poppy, I feel at home. Far more than I do when I'm actually at the hall. It's the best feeling. I can't explain it properly."

He stared into my eyes, and my stomach flipped. There was so much affection there, and I knew it was matched in my own eyes. How could it have taken me so long to see the real man behind all that pomp and circumstance surrounding his family?

In a quiet voice, I said, "You don't have to explain it. I feel so close to you. Strange, isn't it?"

"Not at all," Benedict replied, looking deadly serious.

I had so much to explain. We were only at the beginning of our relationship, but I couldn't go on much longer without telling him my truth. Would he want to spend any more time with a woman who communicated with the dead and called a coven of witches her sisters?

The moment was broken by the arrival of our starters. All three of them. Benedict asked if I'd like a glass of wine. I nodded, intent on fully enjoying myself.

"This looks good," I said, digging in.

Benedict was happily scooping some pork rillettes onto crusty sourdough. I smiled again, enjoying how much *he* was enjoying himself.

If this relationship was going to go anywhere, I had to be honest. I took a sip of wine. I needed courage, every last bit of it. But I had to trust my instinct. And my instincts told me that Benedict was trustworthy. I took a deep breath, hardly believing what I was about to do.

"Benedict," I said.

My tone made him put down his bread. "Oh no. That does not sound good."

"I have something to tell you."

"Yep, that really does not sound good at all. I knew you were too good to be true. Are you married? Boyfriend back home in America?"

I smiled. "No." Could I tell him not to worry? Not really. I was about to divulge something huge. So huge I couldn't believe I was actually about to do it.

"It's about me. Something I never expected to have to tell you."

Benedict stiffened. "You're seeing someone else, aren't you? I knew it. I knew that someone would have already swept you off your feet. I shouldn't have waited to ask you out for as long as I did. I—"

I cut him off with gentle shove to the arm. "Stop it," I said. "Would I accept a date with you if I was seeing someone else?"

The relief on Benedict's face was so tremendous that I immediately knew I was making the right decision. If I was going to let this person into my life, then I had to be honest. We had to start on the right footing.

"It's not another person. More like another aspect to me."

Benedict nodded solemnly.

"Recently I learned something new about myself. Only since I came to Broomewode Village, really." I swallowed. *Here goes*—if he got up and walked straight out of the restaurant, then at least I'd know early on that he couldn't handle the truth about me. I lowered my head but then corrected myself. I needed to be proud of who I was. I looked Benedict straight in the eyes and then said, "It's going to sound strange, and I completely understand that this will be hard to hear."

I took a breath. It was like jumping from a high cliff into water below. Terrifying. I looked into his eyes and stepped off the cliff. "I'm a witch. A water witch, to be exact. I have some special powers that aren't of this world. Powers that I'm just figuring out myself."

There was a beat where I thought I might fall through the floor. And then Benedict smiled and then nodded. *Smiled and nodded!*

"Oh, I thought you might be. There are loads around here, you know."

I felt like I couldn't quite get my breath. Did Benedict just take my deepest secret in his stride? Even a little blasé? I was dumbstruck.

He laughed. "Don't look so surprised. The village is an energy vortex for witches. You know Belinda in the kitchen?"

I nodded, my mouth still open.

"She's a witch, too. Not the most discreet one. Always trying out spells in the kitchen when she thinks no one's watching. They always seem to end in disaster, though. A pot bubbling over and staining the worktops or some kind of smoke explosion." He rolled his eyes.

I couldn't help it—the relief was so great, I burst out laughing.

Benedict joined me, and his smile turned teasing. "So long as whenever you get annoyed with me, we talk things out and you don't turn me into a frog or something."

He was speaking like there was a future for us together. I could feel myself melting.

"I really can't believe you're taking this so well."

But Benedict shrugged like it was nothing and bit into his slice of sourdough. He chewed thoughtfully. I followed his cue and took a bite of chicken. It was delicious. The pine breadcrumb was subtle and provided an unexpected sweetness.

Benedict swallowed. "Might your powers help solve the mystery of Charles's murder? And clear Katie's name?"

I shook my head sadly. "I haven't harnessed their true nature. But my powers are getting stronger. Do you really believe Katie's innocent?"

"There's still a part of me hoping that my father's death was a simple horse-riding accident. Does that sound naïve?"

"Of course not. It's so understandable." I leaned across the table and took his hand. He looked down at our interlaced fingers and smiled.

"Mother's convinced she did it. I didn't know father was planning to fire Katie. That would give her a motive, but the Katie I know would never hurt one of us. So I'm conflicted. All I can do is make sure she has the best defense possible. Unless we can prove she didn't commit the crime."

He sipped his wine. "I don't want our evening to be ruined by speaking of crime, but obviously it's rather on my mind."

"Of course." First his father, now his father's friend, dead in the family vault. Pretty hard for that to slip a person's mind.

"The police interviewed us earlier today, of course. They seemed to be looking for a connection between Katie and Charles Radlier. But Katie'd have no reason to kill Charles. She couldn't have killed him."

"You're forgetting she was out on bail yesterday, awaiting trial. Technically, she could have done it."

Maybe getting Katie out on bail hadn't done her such a favor. Now it looked like Katie could be charged with two murders instead of one.

"She's staying with Eve, so maybe they were together and she has an alibi," I offered, hoping it was enough. "Do they know when Charles Radlier died?" Time of death was always important in these cases.

"I don't know. You need your friend Hamish to find out what the detectives know. They talk to him."

But Hamish was understandably more interested in winning the baking competition than helping solve another murder. At least for this weekend.

"What about other suspects? I heard that Charles was in

debt." I didn't tell him I got the information from a ghost. He'd accepted I was a witch. One step at a time.

Benedict admitted that Charles owed a lot of people a lot of money. "My father suspected he'd been embezzling the hunt money." He looked out over the restaurant. "He was furious. If my father wasn't already dead, I'd have said he was angry enough to kill Charles Radlier."

I tucked into the dressed crab, spooning the creamy, salty mix onto bread. "Could there be someone else as angry as your father about the hunt funds going missing?"

"No one but Father would be as affected."

"And why kill the person who was in debt? Surely that meant there was less chance of getting the money back?" It didn't make sense.

Benedict chewed his food thoughtfully. "But I can't help but think that was my father's jealousy talking. Charles wanted to marry my mother, you know. I don't think he ever got over her. Father did not like it one bit. I didn't mind the man so much, to be honest, but I certainly wouldn't have wanted him as a stepfather."

"Was Charles the only one who had feelings for your mother?" I wondered if he'd mention Harrison Zucker, the financial advisor, or whether that was idle gossip Gerry had overheard.

Benedict put down his fork. "My father's only been dead a week. He's not even buried yet. Are you suggesting—"

"I'm not suggesting anything. Sorry. I got carried away trying to work out who'd have a reason to kill Charles Radlier."

Benedict didn't look happy with this train of thought, but he said, "Harrison Zucker's been spending a lot of time at

Broomewode Hall, but he's there to work. There's a great deal to do, as you can imagine, with Father's passing."

"Of course. That makes sense."

He spoke as though he didn't want to say the words. "I won't pretend that I don't believe Harrison has a great fondness for Mother. As she does for him." He looked concerned. "You think maybe he removed his rival? That would make him a murderer. A murderer who is staying in our home, trying to get close to my mother. I'll have to keep him away from her until we know more."

I shuddered. What a horrible extra worry for Benedict. He'd just lost his father, and now he was worrying about his mother's friends.

We finished our starters, and the waiter returned to clear away the empty plates. We dropped talk of murder, and I asked Benedict more about his childhood, determined to know more about the man I was falling for. Now that I didn't have the burden of my secret, I was free to fall as hard as I wanted to.

What he described wasn't anything like I'd imagined. Yes, there were lavish dinners and balls, long hunting trips in Scotland, vacations in the south of France, polo games, fencing lessons—all the things I imagined a privileged member of the British aristocracy would experience growing up. But that wasn't what Benedict focused on. He talked about being home-schooled as a young boy with a frosty governess, dreaming of going to the local school, only to be sent to a strict boarding school where he lived in fear of his teachers. His fondest memories were with the staff, Katie especially, who'd take him into the village with them on shopping trips. Tasting cheeses at the deli, rich and frothy hot chocolates at the café, helping to choose extravagant bouquets of violets and irises and fragrant eucalyptus at the flower shop. "Everything I know about life," he said, "real life, I learned from the staff. I was never interested in my parents' way of living. It was too concerned with appearances. All etiquette, no soul."

I nodded. The small things he took pleasure in, I shared. In a strange way, we'd both been raised by people who weren't our blood relatives.

Our main courses arrived, and we tucked in greedily, both still famished despite the lovely starters. The beef bourguignon was decadent, tender chunks of meat in a rich red wine gravy nestling tender pearl onions. Benedict laughed as I waxed lyrical about the dish. "I love how you love to eat," he said. "Have you always enjoyed food so much?"

I explained how I'd grown up alongside Gina's family at the Philpott bakery. "Baking was a way of life, and mealtimes were the same. I loved being at Gina's for dinner. Her mom is an excellent cook, and I'd watch her preparing food in the kitchen." I deliberated telling Benedict about Mildred, my kitchen ghost who liked to school me in Victorian delicacies, but decided not to push his threshold for the kooky. All that could come later. Instead, I talked about moving to the States, spending my teenage years by the beach, what high school was like for me, how a part of me always felt that Oregon wasn't home, how I came back to England to study as soon as I could and never left again.

We talked and talked and ate, laughing and holding hands beneath the table. It was the most blissed out I'd been in forever.

Forgoing dessert after such a rich meal, we ordered coffee

and finally stopped to take a breath and surveyed the restaurant. It had half-emptied, and following Benedict's gaze out to the sky, inky-black through the sash windows, I realized it was late.

"The full moon is approaching," he said. "I suppose you'll be busy the rest of the weekend doing witchy things with the full moon."

I gasped. "How did you know about the moon magic circles?"

Benedict grinned. "There's a reason I know there's so many witches in Broomewode, you know. I could never sleep when I was younger. My bedroom was cold and drafty and full of eerie sounds, so I used to sneak out of the hall at night to wander the grounds. One evening, I stumbled on a magic circle and hid behind a tree to watch. A bit naughty, I know, but I knew so many of the women. I have fond memories of that time. There was something so comforting about knowing they were out there, summoning their powers for good. It helped me sleep better. Although I was a bit jealous I didn't have any powers myself."

"You're full of surprises," I said. "It isn't always easy being a witch."

"No. I suppose not, but I envy you all the same."

He leaned over and kissed me full on the lips, soft and tender. I breathed in the scent of him.

Whatever happened, I felt happy that we'd had this beautiful night together.

he next morning, I floated to the baking tent, still
lost in the dreamy quality of my date with Benedict. We'd driven back to Broomewode in the light of the
near-full moon, its silvery orb flooding the Bentley with a
luminous shine. He dropped me back at the inn, and we'd
shared another steamy kiss. When my alarm shrieked its way
through my dreams, I realized I'd only been in bed for five
hours and I had to drag myself downstairs for the early shift. I
baked in a daze, alone in the kitchen and going through the
motions, using a little magic to summon the packets of flour
and sugar to my mixer. Well, if a girl couldn't use her powers
in the kitchen, where could she?

My baking finished, I ate breakfast with Ruta and Pavel
and excused myself to join the crowd I knew would be
outside the baking tent for the first day of the grand finale.

I was still yawning as I climbed the hill and saw how
many people were already at the tent. I shook my head,
wishing I'd left earlier to secure a prime viewing position. As
I got closer, the Florence versus Hamish divide was clear. On

one side, Italian flags were being waved wildly in the air; on the other, the blue and white cross of the Scottish national flag. The tension was palpable, and everyone wanted their favorite to win. Oh, dear. I was going to have to position myself very carefully so as not to give away my true allegiances.

I felt nervous for the bakers. Each week, the challenges grew in difficulty and the pressure fired up. The final episode of the show drew the most home viewers, and Hamish and Florence would be watched by millions worldwide, strangers who had high expectations for their performances, who'd be disappointed if either baker made a foolish mistake. The media, too, were watching, ready to spread the news, ready to highlight the win. It could be cruel out there, and I was worried for both my friends—even Florence. I didn't wish harm on her, even though she was getting on my last nerve with all her boasting and her overtures towards Benedict. But, safe in the knowledge that Benedict had eyes for no one but me, I could be generous. I thought about Benedict again, warmth flooding my sleepy body.

I gazed at the vast expanse of crisp white calico erected across the gorgeous green lawns of the estate. It looked extra bright this morning, as if Broomewode knew that this was its last opportunity to shine. Since the competition wouldn't air for a while yet, there'd been no on-air discussion of the earl's death, though it had appeared in the national media. Benedict had said nice things about his father and thanked all the well-wishers. The countess, predictably, had rushed to assure everyone that "the show would go on."

She might be a countess, but it was Benedict who had all the class in that family.

What would the grounds look like after the tent had been dismantled? The long planks of polished pine taken up and packed away for another year; the white workbenches taken apart and stored. It would certainly change the landscape of Broomewode Village. The weekly crowds of fans would disperse, either jubilant that their favorite had won, or disappointed. They might visit the gift store before leaving, stock up on jams and preserves, buy some of *The Great British Baking Contest's* merchandise—printed T-shirts, mugs and aprons, and hopefully a few copies of Elspeth and Jonathon's respective cookbooks.

I made my way through the crowd to the front to give the bakers a good-luck wave. The crew were buzzing about the tent at double speed, checking mics and lights and camera angles. It was all go go go. My heart quickened in sympathy for the final two (though really it was for Hamish) and the nerves they must be experiencing as the clock ticked. I stared at the two workstations at the front of the tent where Hamish and Florence would battle it out. They gleamed, supplies labeled and arranged, pencils sharpened and waiting to be used. Everything was yet to come.

Hamish and Florence appeared and came to the front to greet their fans. Florence waved to them like royalty, emulating the queen's subtle turn of the wrist. She looked incredible, her hair carefully styled. Perfect black flicks elongated her eyes, and she fluttered what must have been fake lashes at the crowd, smiling with candy-pink lips.

Hamish was his usual down-to-earth self in a short-sleeved shirt and dark jeans. Rather than a royal wave, he thanked everyone for coming and then ducked back inside the tent, no doubt to go over his notes one final time. I knew he'd be feeling the pressure the most.

Jilly and Arty emerged from the other path. They were hand in hand, abandoning any concealment of their burgeoning romance. I smiled and waved at them, knowing that we shared the same loved-up flush. A calm came over me, and I knew that Elspeth and Jonathon weren't far behind the comedians. I wanted to talk to Elspeth about Benedict so badly, but would she be angry that I had revealed my witch status so quickly? I'd never give away another witch's identity, but would she feel protective about our shared secret and admonish me? I'd so hate to upset Elspeth.

And then there she was, my witchy godmother, looking gorgeous in a pearl-colored suit. Jonathon looked relaxed in dark jeans and navy shirt. In fact, his whole demeanor was more relaxed than usual. Could it be that he was relieved that filming was coming to an end? It must take a toll being on-camera during the weekend, and word on the street was that Jonathon was hounded by moms with crushes the rest of the time.

Eve had told me how he couldn't even pop to the super-market without being asked for his autograph or even for a cheeky date. Jonathon was said to be a confirmed bachelor, but I couldn't imagine him staying single for long. Surely he wanted to have someone to cook for, go on long rambles through the countryside with. Or was I just falling prey to the love bug? I smiled at them both and waved.

There was a flurry of activity in the tent, and before long the director, Fiona, was calling for quiet and the cameras began to roll. The signature challenge was up first, and I realized that this week I had no idea what it was. All our chat had been about the final showstopper. I leaned forward to hear Jonathon introduce the challenge, feeling the true excitement of a viewer. It was banquet week, but what would count as a signature banquet bake? I had no idea. As Jonathon explained how the theme would showcase various techniques used to create bakes good enough for a historical banquet, I hung on every syllable until I heard the words "twelve mini eclairs."

The cameras went to Hamish first, who already looked sick with nerves, all the color drained from his face. He explained to Jonathon that he was making salted caramel and coffee cream eclairs. He knew that his greatest challenge was going to be keeping each eclair identical in size and finished to a level that would be delicate and presentable on a silver banquet plate. "I like the sound of your flavor combinations, Hamish," Jonathon said kindly. "Robust and satisfying. Just make sure you don't let the coffee take over. Elspeth is more of a tea kind of lady. She can't take the caffeine—sends her all of a twitter."

"Can't be disappointing Elspeth at this stage," Hamish said, trying to smile.

"Very smart," Jonathon said approvingly.

Elspeth was cued to walk towards Florence, who I knew would be feeling in her element with choux pastry. She also had an eye for detail and wrote the very book on finesse. It was difficult for me to watch how well Florence handled the mini-interview. She was charming, funny, didn't take herself too seriously, and not one bit of nerves showed through. She knew exactly what she was doing, and not even the questioning of the great Elspeth Peach could shake Florence.

"Choux is a very traditional French pastry, but of course I've tinkered around, adding an Italian twist to this classic."

Florence's fans silently waved their Italian flags in solidarity. I tried to appreciate how good she was and not feel irked that she might soon have a TV show with Benedict's mother.

"But I also wanted to make this bake modern. I wanted to play with the shape and color, so there's a few surprises in store today."

"Can you explain what you're doing at the moment?" Elspeth asked, gesturing at Florence's pan.

"Of course. I've cooked my panade, that's the butter and flour and liquid. I've used milk. Now I add my eggs one at a time and beat them into the dough."

Elspeth was nodding along approvingly. "Your dough is a fantastic color."

"It's the egg yolks. They're from the local farm here in Broomewode Village and are the best eggs I've ever used. They're creamy and rich and delicious." She chef-kissed her hands.

Well, at least Florence had the decency to credit Susan's farm with the eggs. I peered over at Hamish's workstation to see if he was listening to Florence's spiel, but his head was down, concentrating.

But Florence wasn't finished with the cameras yet. While the mixer was doing its thing, she turned the full force of her attention on Elspeth and explained her piping technique. "I learned early on that you can't put too much pressure on the bag while piping," she said. "The dough is quite liquid, so if you squeeze too much, then you can't get the delicate shape I'm after. Once baked, they should be smooth on top but crispy as well."

Florence flashed her lovely smile, and Elspeth wished her good luck.

Argh. It was difficult to watch her be so charming. But to my horror, someone else was as frustrated as me—and seemingly about to take it out in the best way he knew how. Gerry was steadily floating his way over to Florence's workstation, a determined look on that pallid ghostly face of his.

I stepped forward and held my breath. I'd already warned Gerry not to get involved today. How could I communicate to Gerry that he needed to scram? Vamoose? Get gone? I tried to get his attention by staring hard, but if he felt my bad vibes, then he certainly wasn't showing it. I watched, frustration mounting, as he began to use his paranormal powers to lift Florence's piping bag. Was he going to attempt to interfere? Surely not. But yes. It began to slide, achingly slowly, across the workstation towards the floor.

Argh, Gerry was insufferable. Did he leave his listening skills in the living world when he got electrocuted? It was unethical to interfere with the show. Unconscionable! I couldn't let it happen. But the only alternative was to use my own powers. It couldn't count as using them for my own gain if, in fact, I was stopping the sabotage about to be enacted on someone I would happily see lose the competition—right?

I closed my eyes and focused on the piping bag. In my mind's eye, I could see the whole worksurface clearly. The neatly arranged ingredients, the bowl, the mixer. With all the force I could muster, I began to concentrate on moving the piping bag away from the edge. Energy flooded my body, and I could feel myself begin to flush. *Focus, Pops, focus.* I opened my eyes. It was working! The piping bag had stopped moving —inches away from the edge.

Florence, who'd been busy cutting sheets of baking paper, now turned to find her precious dough-filled bag awfully close to the edge. She frowned, and I could tell she was wondering how she'd been so clumsy as to leave it in such a precarious position. If Gerry could have turned red, he would have in that moment. He took his attention away from Florence and searched the crowd. We locked eyes, and I shook my head at him, furious.

Florence continued with her schedule and Hamish his. The cameras followed their every move, intent on recording each moment.

Gerry floated over to me. "How could you?" he said in a voice more befitting a toddler.

Of course, I couldn't reply. We were in the middle of a crowd with countless cameras mere yards away. Gerry took this opportunity to berate me without rebuke. I had no choice but to listen while he tried to justify his actions, that a little spilled dough wasn't the end of the world but enough to slow Florence down.

But no amount of reasoning could make me think his actions were justified. I could feel my blood boiling. I wanted to tell Gerry that with special powers came responsibilities. We had an obligation to be fair and just. We couldn't mess with people on a whim.

I slipped away from the crowd and gestured for Gerry to follow me.

As soon as we were out of earshot, I let him have it. In fairness to Gerry, he didn't even try to interrupt me as I gathered momentum, lecturing him with echoes of the wise words Elspeth had once given to me.

As soon as I paused for breath, Gerry opened his mouth.

"Yeah, yeah, I get you, Pops, but you've got to lighten up. It was horseplay. It's not like I tried to add salt instead of sugar to her bowl."

I stopped pacing the rose garden and stared at Gerry. "Tell me that you're only joking and that you didn't do that."

Gerry busied himself lifting a yellow rose to his nose and sniffing it. I didn't know what for—ghosts had no sense of smell or taste. "Gerry?"

He looked up with an impish smile on his face. "No, I didn't. But I was seriously considering it until you got in my way."

I'd have smacked him, but what was the point? I'd feel as though I'd swung my hand through a refrigerator and he'd laugh at me.

"You're such a stern schoolmistress these days. If we can't have a little fun, then what's the point of it all?"

"Gerry, you haven't been listening to a word I've said." I took a breath and tried to calm myself down. "Promise me you won't interfere again."

"But I'm so bored."

"There's no buts here." I now acted like a stern schoolmistress, putting my hands on my hips and glaring at him.

"Okay, I promise," Gerry mumbled. "But you are not in my good books, Poppy Wilkinson."

"Right back at you," I said.

To my surprise, Gerry flounced off in the direction of the inn without so much as a goodbye. Well, at least he wasn't going back to the tent. I'd managed to avert disaster, at least for now.

I knew he was frustrated that he didn't seem able to cross

over. He was stuck here at Broomewode, and it made him act out. If only I could help him move on. One more task to add to an overwhelming list that included solving a murder.

Sure, Charles Radlier was nothing to me, but Benedict was involved, and if I could do anything to make his life easier, I was going to do it.

CHAPTER 11

I wasn't flouncing off like Gerry, but I found I was too tense to watch the competition. I needed a break. And a coffee.

Back at the inn, it was quiet.

I entered the pub, desperate for a coffee and to talk with Eve. I wanted to share everything about my date last night with someone who'd understand what it meant to tell my secret, but before I found Eve, I caught sight of DI Hembly and Sgt. Lane sitting at a table with Trim, the reporter from *Broomewode News.* They looked to be deep in conversation, and I doubted it had anything to do with the baking competition.

Now how to interrupt without looking like I was sleuthing around?

Maybe I could offer to get them all coffee since I needed some myself. I went over to their table, but before I even suggested coffee, Adam Lane invited me to take a seat. He knew my game. "We're going back over Trim's photos from the hunt. You could be useful. You were there."

This was almost better than coffee. "You're trying to find a link between the earl and the Master of the Hunt's deaths?"

DI Hembly said, "We're looking at many possibilities, but it is strange that both the earl and Charles Radlier, the Master of the Hunt, should be killed within a week and Mr. Radlier placed in the Champney family vault."

Trim said, "I took a mountain of photos. Maybe something here will help."

Hembly's eyebrows rose. We all knew that Trim was ambitious and hoping to turn his access to these murder cases to good account in getting a higher profile job.

He spread photos over the table. Horses in flight, elegant faces in the crowd, details of the traditional outfits—shining buckles and fancy hats. Families following the hunt over the rolling hills of Broomewode. The hounds running around looking important.

"Wait," I said. "Let's take a closer look at that one." I pointed at a photograph of a horse. The foreground was of the horse standing good-naturedly while a little girl stroked its nose, but I saw something else. "See there? In the background? Isn't that Charles Radlier? He doesn't look happy. Who's that with him?"

Trim got out a magnifying glass and studied the photo. "It's Charles Radlier and Harrison Zucker," Trim replied. He glanced up. "Well spotted, Poppy."

"In the midst of an argument. Look at their red faces." I squinted. "Harrison is clenching his fist." I was elated at my find. After Gerry overheard Radlier was in debt, I'd been wanting to find a way to lead the detectives to water, so to speak, but of course I couldn't have given away the source, and I didn't want to have to pretend I'd overheard the gossip myself. Lying (even white lies from a white witch) to the police seemed like a bad idea.

Hembly nodded. "I noticed Mr. Zucker was paying a lot of attention to Evelyn Frome at her husband's funeral."

I'd been so focused on Florence paying attention to Lady Frome that I hadn't really registered who else had offered her a comforting shoulder.

"Perhaps we need to pay him a visit, sir," Lane suggested.

I was happy the detectives had made the link themselves.

"Does that mean Katie's no longer a suspect?" I asked.

Hembly firmly but politely told me to butt out of police business.

I nodded, but come on—as if.

They stood, thanked Trim for his photos and what Lane called my "beady eye" and went off in search of Harrison Zucker. Naturally, they'd find him at Broomewode.

I was overjoyed the police had found a new lead and the heat might be off Katie Donegal. We still had some unfinished business, she and I, and I decided that coffee could wait. I'd pop in at Eve's and see the disgraced Broomewode cook. My gushing to Eve about Benedict would have to wait.

Eve said Katie would be glad of the company and gave me directions to her flat. I'd never been to Eve's place before. She explained it was a small two-bed above the flower shop on the edge of Broomewode Village. "You have to press hard on the buzzer twice, luvvie, otherwise it doesn't work. Plus, Katie doesn't have the sharpest hearing in town. Though she'd be mad with me for saying it."

I laughed. "Katie does like to think she has her ear to the ground at all times."

Eve kissed my cheeks and told me to be safe in the village.

She checked my wrist for her amulet and smiled when she found it twinkling beneath the cuffs of my blue linen shirt. I asked her to feed Gateau if she ever resurfaced from her nap and took a small bundle of leftover breakfast muffins for Katie.

SETTING off for the other side of the village, I kept my eye on the blue skies above me, hoping to catch a glimpse of the hawk. He hadn't been spotted since last week, and I couldn't figure out if that was a good or bad sign. On the one hand, he appeared when danger was nearby. On the other, the bird was connected to my birth dad, and when I saw him swooping through the skies, I felt comfort. Protected.

I picked up my pace and made my way along the pretty residential streets, admiring the blooming gardens and neatly trimmed lawns of the cottages. I crossed through the village green away from the parade of shops I knew so well. There was the deli, the tea shop, the butcher's, the greengrocers, and the antique store, whose window displays always tempted me. The streets were busier than usual, young families making use of the little park, everyone enjoying the weather now that the rain had passed.

I turned into Eve's street and immediately saw the swinging brass sign for the florist she lived above. "Angel's Blooms" it said in bold block letters, the outline of a rose carved beside it. The window display was a beautiful sight: scarlet tinge of peonies, buttery freesias, purple alliums, green foliage piled high and spilling from buckets. Birds were perched on the rooftop and chirped merrily. I peered through the window and saw a young woman behind the counter, phone balanced between shoulder and ear, writing in a notepad. Roses climbed the side of the building.

To the left of the shop was another door, and I pressed the buzzer beside Eve's name. A few moments later the buzzer crackled into life. "Hello?" a small voice said. Usually Katie was blustery and warm and full of beans. It pained me to hear her so obviously shrunken. I said my name, that I came bearing pastries, and Katie perked up immediately.

"How nice. I'll buzz you in, dearie."

The door didn't move. I pushed against it, but still it didn't budge.

"Come in, come in," Katie's voice insisted.

I laughed. "I'm trying, believe me."

Katie mumbled something about modern technology, and the buzzer made a sharp noise of protest. Bless Katie's cotton socks. She couldn't figure out an intercom—how did the police think she could plan and carry out a murder plot on her wealthy boss?

"Now I just press this thingie with that thingie... Aha."

The door gave way, and I entered into a dim hallway carpeted in mauve and climbed the stairs.

Katie was waiting at the top. Unlike when I invited myself into her cottage to see Mitty, she was happy to see me. Deprived of her Broomewode Hall uniform, she was dressed casually in mustard slacks and a white shirt, her gray hair freshly washed and still drying. Her cheeks, however, didn't have their usual rosy glow, and her brown eyes were heavy with a deep sadness.

Overcome with empathy for her recent plight, I pulled

Katie close to me and gave her a squeeze. "So glad they've released you," I said into her ear.

Katie seemed like she couldn't believe her plight. She thanked me and walked me inside Eve's flat. It was cozy, as I'd known it would be, but with modern furniture and finishes and an open-plan living area. A large gray couch dominated the space, and a glass coffee table was piled high with books. The walls were painted sage green, and the whole place was full of potted plants. I mean everywhere. All shapes and sizes proudly gathered in the corners, others hanging from hooks and trickling down walls like green waterfalls. I guessed Eve must have a good relationship with the store downstairs and went wild. I loved it. The whole place felt like a slice of nature indoors.

Katie told me to take a seat while she put on a pot of tea, and I chose one of two rocking chairs that faced each other by the window. Light poured through the sash windows. It was so peaceful up here, exactly the kind of place Eve would need to return to after a long shift at the inn.

Katie clattered around in the kitchen, arranging the muffins I'd brought on a plate, and then came to join me. "This is my favorite spot, too," she said, handing me a cup and saucer.

"Verbena," Katie said. "Eve doesn't seem to believe in ordinary tea. So many herbal ones in there. You wouldn't believe the selection. This is her favorite."

I thanked her and took a sip of the hot liquid. It smelled and tasted balmy and healing. I could see why Eve liked it.

"I'm sorry to have missed the funeral yesterday," Katie said abruptly. "I wanted to be there with every ounce of my being, to pay my respects to the earl." She shook her head.

"The countess, I think maybe she's unraveled since the earl's death. It's the only conclusion that makes sense. Why she imagines I'd have anything to do with his death, I can't work out. I've worked for their family for the best part of my life. I'd do anything for them. But no one believes that note was meant for Derek. They're convinced I was threatening the earl." Katie's eyes filled with tears again. "All this over an argument about the price of sausages. I wish I'd kept my cool with that nasty, gouging butcher and not let myself get so worked up. How could I have known it would get me into this spot? You've no idea how many times I've cursed my hot temper. I've always been that way, ever since I was a wee baby. My old ma used to tell me that one day my wagging tongue would get me into trouble. She was so right." Her voice trembled. "They think I killed the earl. I could go to jail."

"But you've got a good lawyer, and you have plenty of people trying to find out the truth." I thought that was diplomatic. I was one of those. Whatever the truth was, I wanted to find it, but if Katie had killed the earl, she would have to pay for her crime.

"And now I hear poor Charles Radlier is dead." She seemed like her world was falling in. "One tragedy after another."

"Did you know him well?" Of course, Katie probably knew of the Master of the Hunt even if she didn't know him personally.

Katie nodded. "Just from the lordship's parties. Nothing more personal than that. Eve told me about you finding his body. I couldn't quite get my head round it. You heard noises down there?"

I clung to my story about having good hearing, being in the right spot, and the door being open.

"I can't explain it," I found myself saying. "But I heard noises. Or I thought I did."

"The rats." Katie nodded. "Eve told me about how bad they are down there. Seems she heard them too."

Phew. Thank goodness for Eve. "Exactly. But also, I had a hunch."

"Your instincts are good, Poppy," Katie said, a little whimsically. "You pick up on the subtlest clues and don't let go. It's something which you were born with."

I set down my tea. What was Katie saying?

"My poor Benedict," she continued, dropping whatever train of thought had struck. "He must have had an awful morning of it. Preparing to bury his father and then suddenly —more murder, more disruption. No funeral." She bit into a blueberry muffin.

It was terrible to hear those words from Katie's lips. In essence, although I wasn't to blame for Charles Radlier's murder, I had been the orchestrator of his father's ruined funeral. Suddenly, there was a strange scrambling noise, not unlike the one I'd faked hearing at the funeral.

"What is that?" I said to Katie. "Some kind of rustling?"

Katie chuckled. "Oh, you do have good hearing! That's Frankie."

Had Katie's time in remand messed with her mind?

"Frankie?"

Katie stood and disappeared into another room. "You're going to love this," she called out.

Was I? What was Katie doing?

She returned, all coy, holding something carefully in her arms like a baby.

"Poppy, meet Frankie."

Katie was holding a rabbit. An extremely cute, gray rabbit, his nose twitching and his furry bottom wriggling in Katie's grasp.

"Lord knows what possessed Eve to want a rabbit as a pet," she said, "but I must admit I've grown quite fond of him already." She stroked his soft head, and Frankie quietened in her arms.

Of *course* Eve had an animal at home—it was her familiar. "Don't tell Gateau," I whispered to Frankie, "but I think you might be the most adorable little thing I've seen in a while."

Frankie twitched his nose, and Katie settled him on the floor, where he began to explore.

Katie washed up and then brought over muffins. I accepted a lemon and poppy seed muffin and tasted it critically, as I'd begun to taste all baking. Even my own. It was an occupational hazard. I couldn't taste every batch of baking I made, so it was nice to find that the muffins tasted good. I hadn't realized how hungry I was. It was nearing lunchtime, and I was ready to eat.

Katie nodded. She was playing with her fingers, looping them together and worrying her fingernails. "And my Mitty? How is he? It's been all kinds of dreadful not being able to see him every day. "

I swallowed. I didn't want to tell Katie that Mitty had been acting strange at the funeral. But maybe she could help me sort fuddled memory from truth. I told Katie that Mitty had been confused, mixing up Robert Champney's death with the previous viscount, Stephen Champney, his cousin. "Second cousin," she said. I found it interesting that these two old retainers were so determined to put that extra distance between the man who should have been the Earl of Frome and the one who got the job by default. "Mitty was fixated on the day Stephen Champney went over the cliff. Talking about poachers and Robert Champney being out on the grounds spooking the horse. He said, in a very loud voice, that it wasn't an accident." I didn't tell her that the countess had been furious. No doubt she'd figure that out herself.

Katie looked down at her tea. Was she avoiding my gaze?

"Katie? Does Mitty talk about that with you as well? Is there any truth to his ramblings?"

Katie cleared her throat. "Mitty says a lot of things. His mind isn't what it was."

"His memory might not be working in a linear way, but that doesn't mean he's making things up. Was Robert Champney out riding the day the viscount died?"

Frankie shuffled over and wanted attention. I set down my tea and stroked his soft ears. I waited, but my usually chatty companion didn't answer my question.

"Katie?"

But a jangling sound turned both our attentions to the door. A key was being turned in the lock. Surely Eve couldn't have left the inn already? She was mid-shift.

Katie's cheeks pinkened, and she half-rose as the door opened.

And in walked 'Joanna.' Or the woman who'd introduced herself to me as Joanna.

I don't know who was more shocked, me to find Joanna walking into Eve's house or Joanna to find me there.

For a second, no one said a word. I felt the woman considering whether to turn around and leave and was ready to stop her with magic if necessary. Then she seemed to accept the inevitable and came all the way inside.

I looked at her and then Katie. "What is going on?" I demanded, anger rising in me. Joanna had given me the runaround for a week, and now here she was, letting herself into Eve's apartment?

Silence. Even Frankie stopped halfway to Joanna.

Joanna looked sick with fear.

Finally, Katie spoke. "It's time you told her, dear."

CHAPTER 12

*T*ime stopped.

  If I'd been a better witch, I would have sworn that it was me casting a spell to freeze the moment. Joanna opened and then closed her mouth and stayed by the door. She looked exactly as she had when we met last week. Shiny blond hair cut into a thick, chin-length bob. Square champagne-colored glasses, warm brown eyes. And the same look of terror was etched on her face as when the tractor headed towards us in the café. I'd never had that effect on a person before.

  Katie settled back in her rocking chair, her hand still clutching half a muffin. Were the seconds ticking past? It seemed impossible to tell. I couldn't wrap my mind around what I was seeing. But a deep sense of betrayal was bubbling inside me, and the pain of it was too much to bear.

  Frankie broke the moment when he resumed hopping his way over to Joanna. She bent down and picked him up. He snuffled, contented. I got the feeling he knew this woman well. More than I could say.

"I expect you have a lot of questions for me, Poppy," Joanna said.

Oh, she had that right. I stood up and placed my hands on my hips. I wanted to shout and scream at this woman. Why had she disappeared on me? Who was she? What was with all the secrecy? And what was she doing in Broomewode?

"I'm going to pop out for a bit of fresh air," Katie said. And with that she disappeared from the room. It was no surprise —the tension between us was palpable, and Katie clearly knew something I didn't. As usual. As much as I liked Katie, she'd been giving me the runaround since day one.

Joanna told me to sit, and I obeyed, even though every fiber of my being wanted to rally against this infuriating woman. But as Joanna and Frankie came towards me and took Katie's chair, I began to calm down. Like all the way down. It was like Joanna was coating me in a soothing balm, removing the red flashing behind my eyes, softening my heartbeat, my tense muscles.

She was a witch. Definitely. A powerful one.

"Who *are* you?" I said, trying to summon back my gumption.

Joanna settled back in her seat. She took a deep breath, gathering herself. The suspense was killing me.

"Well, I'm not Joanna, but I think you've already worked that one out."

I shook my head and repeated the question. "I know who you're not. So why don't we start with who you actually *are*?"

"Joanna" leaned forward in her chair and placed Frankie on the floor. He scuttled away. She looked at me, and her gaze was sad. "I think, deep down, you know."

There was so much warmth suffusing my body now I

couldn't speak. I could only nod. As I watched, "Joanna" took off her square glasses. Then she put a hand to her head and pulled at the crown of her hair. The wig came away in her hands. Brunette waves tumbled to her shoulders. My mouth fell open. Now I could see the resemblance she'd been trying to hide.

It was like I was seeing clearly for the first time in my life.

"Valerie," I breathed.

She nodded solemnly, and her kind eyes filled with tears. "Poppy, my Poppy."

She came to me then and pulled me into her arms. "Poppy. I'm so sorry I left you." Confusion and anger and love swirled in me. How had I been so blind? She was here all along. I'd seen her, I'd met her, I'd talked with her—and yet...

"Why?" I said, pulling away suddenly, shrugging her away from my body. "Why all the mystery? What was the point in hiding yourself from me? I don't understand how you could lie. For all those years. I mean, I'm your *daughter.*"

Valerie hung her head. I could see now that her hair was the same shade of brown as mine. No wonder Mitty had called me Valerie. We weren't identical, but he'd known Valerie when she was my age. He'd seen the resemblance.

"We look alike," I murmured.

And then I was furious again with Katie. For weeks and weeks, I'd been asking Katie about a woman named Valerie. She'd pretended to barely remember her, then conceded she recalled someone of that name and then that she'd left Broomewode without a word. Yet she was here, all that time. In Broomewode. Valerie. My mom.

"Let me explain," she said softly.

I didn't reply, not trusting myself to speak.

She opened her mouth and then closed it again. "I can't get over how much you look like I did when I was your age."

I stared at her and realized I was holding my breath. Despite myself, I was softening. "My heart recognized you straightaway when I saw you in the café last week. I just wasn't open to what I was really seeing."

Valerie nodded and took a deep breath. "I'm your mother, Poppy. I've kept up with you secretly all of your life. Every key moment, I reached across oceans with my powers and I've seen you. I've been *with* you. I was so young when I discovered I was pregnant with you. I was scared. Life in Broomewode was so complicated. You can't even begin to imagine. But the minute I saw your tiny face, those wide innocent eyes, that sweet tuft of dark hair on your head, I loved you and I had to keep you safe."

I touched my fingers to my cheek and was surprised to find them wet.

"You're a witch, too," I managed to murmur. "The connection between us—it's so strong. I felt you from so far away."

"Oh yes. It comes from me. But before I explain any more, you have to understand that I left you with the Philpotts for your own safety. It broke my heart to let you go." Her voice broke on the words.

She paused there, and I remembered my vision of Valerie leaving me at the door of the bakery, hiding behind a tree until I was discovered by Mr. Philpott. I had felt her heart break in that moment, all of her sadness, and I'd pitied my mom during that vision. She had been a woman on the edge, left with no choices. I could feel all of that, yet I still didn't know the story. I wanted to ask more now, but I could see she was in pain.

"And I was right to protect you that way," she continued. "Just look at what happened to us last week."

Wait, this was a huge jump from leaving me in an apple box twenty-five years ago. I felt stunned. "Are you talking about the tractor accident last week?"

"I don't think that was an accident. I'm terrified for us. They want us out of here."

I wasn't certain how close Katie was, but I lowered my voice to a whisper. "The police suspect Katie may have let that tractor go to hurt the earl, never meaning to cause so much damage and presumably not intending to nearly kill us."

She shook her head. "I'm certain Katie had nothing to do with the tractor. I felt the darkness, the evil. That's what caused me to glance up at that moment."

"You sensed it coming? With your powers, I mean. You leapt across that table and threw me to the floor. You saved my life."

I had so many questions, I didn't know where to start. Valerie's own sadness was merging with mine, and I felt her regret as if it were my own. Still, she smiled a little. "I've been trying to save your life for weeks. You're as stubborn as—" She stopped herself, and I wondered how that sentence would have finished naturally. *You're as stubborn as your father?* I was determined to find out who that might be and before too long, but I felt like we had to stay with one part of the story at a time. It was all so much, I felt like my head was going to explode. Or maybe my heart.

"It was you writing me those warning notes, telling me to leave Broomewode Village. They were so threatening. You worried me."

She nodded. "And yet you're still here." She sounded like a mom now, with that scolding tone. "You must see now that you're not safe. That you have to leave for the same reasons I did."

"What reasons?"

This was so frustrating. She had lied to me, lied to my face. Calling herself Joanna, hiding her true identity. Leaving me warning notes, coming to me in eerie unfinished visions that disguised her face. It wasn't fair. How could I trust her? She'd told me my birth mom was living in Glasgow, for goodness' sake. I would have gone on a wild goose chase across the country if I'd followed her advice.

As if she could read my mind, Valerie said softly, "I know this is a lot to take in. You've been searching for me, and I've made myself elusive. You must believe me when I say it was for your own good. My witch's instinct knows that this is a bad place for you, Poppy. It was a bad place for me."

"But why?"

The words hung in the air. I knew it was to do with my birth dad, but I was scared to ask. He was dead. Something tragic had happened. I felt it in my heart, and I saw it in Valerie's face. Was my life really in danger? Aside from the tractor episode, things were going well here. I told Valerie that my life was good. I wanted to tell my mom everything.

She smiled then, a genuine, warm smile that made my heart hurt.

"I love my job, my friends, and my coven sisters here. I have a life." I couldn't keep my new romance a secret one more second. "And I'm seeing someone."

Valerie's eyes widened. "You have a boyfriend? How did I miss that?"

I admitted it was recent. But it felt serious. It was so nice to be girl-talking with my mom, I almost forgot I was angry with her. "Benedict's nothing like I thought he was. He's... amazing. I feel so much like myself with him."

But the smile on Valerie's face vanished. "Benedict? Not Benedict Champney?"

I nodded. "I know we come from different worlds, but it feels right. I can't explain it."

The color drained from Valerie's face, and she stood up and turned to the window. With her back to me, she looked just like the young woman I'd seen in my visions. She rested her forehead on the windowpane for a moment before turning back to me. "I'm sorry, Poppy, but Benedict is all wrong for you. Break it off now before you get hurt."

"What are you talking about?"

"Oh, darling. I wish I could explain."

Now I stood, too. She was still holding out on me. Despite everything. "You can explain. You have to. You owe me an explanation."

"Please, trust my instincts. My powers are more developed than yours, Poppy."

Oh great, now she was going to take a swipe at my powers? That was a low blow. If she'd stayed with me in Broomewode, maybe it wouldn't have taken me so long to discover I was a witch. But I couldn't bring myself to say these words. There was obviously something more behind her warning.

She repeated again that I must trust her. I was so frustrated I wanted to throw something. I'd finally found my mother but I wasn't getting the answers I needed.

"Why don't we leave together? Right now. We can drive back to your place and pack a bag."

I shook my head. What was she talking about? I had no real reason to leave. "I can't. My life is here. My job, my friends." I swallowed. I wasn't going to mention Benedict again. "It's the final weekend of the baking competition. I have to stay at least for the weekend." I had no intention of running away with Valerie on Monday, but at least I could buy myself some time. I wanted her to stick around so I could ask her all the questions. So many questions. I was worried she'd disappear again if I didn't let her believe I'd leave with her just because she said I should.

My phone buzzed in my pocket. It was Hamish. I'd promised to meet him and Florence in the pub once filming was over. He was wondering where I was. I couldn't believe it was so late in the day already.

"I have a thousand questions for you," I said.

"And I promise to answer them." I stood up and then looked at my mother, unsure what to do.

"Meet me tomorrow?" Valerie asked quietly. "If you come back here, I'll send Katie off for a visit with Mitty. She'll talk for hours with that sweet old man, and we can have time alone. We'll talk properly then. I promise. No more running away. I'll be prepared this time. Prepared to tell you everything I know." She glanced at my face, and I could see she was conflicted. "It won't be easy. For either of us."

I had no reason to trust Valerie, but I agreed. I wanted to speak to her away from prying eyes or ears. There was a lifetime of questions to be answered, and I was sick of all these vague warnings, frankly.

She walked me to the door. "Blessed be," she said softly, taking my hands.

I looked at her for a moment, still in shock that it had happened—I'd found my birth mom. Or rather, she'd been watching me all along. It was thrilling and confusing in equal measure. But the feel of her soft, warm skin against mine and the connection between us was enough for me to know intuitively that she cared. She wasn't going to disappear again. I could take this evening to gather my thoughts and order my questions.

"Blessed be," I replied.

She kissed my cheeks, and then I pulled her to me. Valerie. My mom.

I turned and began to walk down the stairs in a daze.

"Poppy? Just a minute."

I spun round. Valerie joined me on the stairs, pressing a box into my hands. "Some happy eggs from Susan Bentley. Pass them on to Hamish for tomorrow with her affection."

I stared at Valerie. How did she know about the happy eggs? About Hamish?

She smiled at me. "I told you, Poppy. I've been keeping up with you. Now take these and promise me you'll keep your wits about you. Take great care. This can be a dangerous place."

And talk about stating the obvious.

CHAPTER 13

I was in a daze. Who could I really trust? Why had Katie been concealing things from me? Why was my birth mom at Eve's when Eve knew all about my long and difficult search? What kind of sister was Eve to keep my own mother from me? I was angry and confused but also, strangely, full of love. My mom. My beautiful mom. She was here. Here!

Part of me was kicking myself because I didn't say all the things I might have said or asked what I might have asked. What was I scared of knowing? I consoled myself that when we met tomorrow, a moment would come which would seem right. I would choose my words carefully. She'd warned me it would be a difficult conversation, and I had no trouble believing it. I suspected my father was dead, and Valerie still needed to explain why she'd abandoned her newborn baby. Me.

Like Valerie, I needed time to prepare.

I arrived back at the inn without remembering how I'd gotten there. My only solace—Gateau waiting for me by the front steps. I picked her up and snuggled into her soft black fur. Hamish's text had given away nothing, only that he was back at the inn and ready for a drink. I hoped beyond hope that he'd pulled it out of the bag for the afternoon's technical challenge. I couldn't deal with any more gloating from Florence.

I pushed through the doors to the pub and scanned the room. At one table sat Florence with her suave producer side-kick. They were drinking champagne again and talking to one another with an intensity and exuberance that made my heart sink. Hamish hadn't pulled it together this afternoon. Clearly Florence had won the second bake, too.

Hamish was on his own, gloomily staring into a pint. Any jolly pretense at togetherness had been dropped completely. Those two were pitted against one another now—it was too hard for them to pretend otherwise. I wished it wasn't the case, that Florence was still the warm sweetheart she'd been when we first met. All smiles and instant friendship. I missed the camaraderie and how welcoming and fun she'd been. It had been easy to get caught up in Florence's personality. She was so effervescent. But now I could only see her ambition and that she'd let nothing get in the way of what she wanted.

Unfortunately, being crowned the country's best baker wasn't enough. She also had her sights set on Benedict Champney, a man I cared for deeply. Her desire was misplaced, born from all the wrong reasons, I was sure. For all those reasons, I had zero inclination to join Florence in her smug win. I went straight to Hamish, arranging my features into some semblance of a smile, ready to buoy him up and make him believe he could still take the win.

As I took a seat, my friend shook his head. "I let my nerves get the better of me," he said. "I think my strength in this competition has always been that I only did it for fun, always expecting every weekend would be my last. But I've made it so far." He glanced at the smug Florence and took another drink of his beer.

I reminded Hamish that all he needed was a spectacular showstopper tomorrow and the win could still be his.

"You know, Poppy, I never cared an ounce about winning before. But Florence is growing more full of herself by the minute. She's already acting like *she's* Elspeth Peach. Without the talent or charm."

I had to agree. Florence was becoming insufferable. He had my vote, for sure, which I suppose I'd made plain by sitting with him instead of the overconfident Italian. Hamish asked if I'd go to watch him tomorrow, as it'd help him focus, and I agreed immediately. It was rare for me to have a Sunday off work now, and what better way to spend it than supporting my friend? I could see Valerie in the afternoon, hopefully with my head clear.

Hamish said he'd get us a drink from the bar and a dinner menu. I was grateful, as I didn't want to talk to Eve yet. I was too angry and confused at her behavior. Why had she let Valerie stay at her place and hide it from me? I didn't know, and I really wasn't in the mood for any more confrontation or surprises.

With Hamish at the bar, I took in the rest of the pub with pleasure. Other people were enjoying an ordinary Saturday evening, sharing wine, frothy pints of ale, and Ruta's excellent food. A spaniel lay obediently down beside a chair and fell straight to sleep. Snippets of conversation carried across the pub. Quiet laughter. Some loud questioning, two people talking over one another. A young family were on their dessert course, tucking into the chocolate cake I'd made earlier and ice cream. Gerry was floating around, of course. He pretended to eat the kids' ice cream. He pulled the dog's ears, and it growled in its sleep. I hoped my goofy ghostly friend was also eavesdropping on all the many conversations in the pub. Somebody must know something about the recent murder. And maybe someone knew something about the earl's death that might prove Katie innocent. Philly was working hard, taking orders, clearing plates, and keeping the water jugs topped up.

An older couple were playing backgammon in the corner. I smiled at Hamish as he returned with my red wine. There was true friendship here, and I was glad of it.

If Florence noticed I was sitting with her last remaining competitor, pretty much stating my allegiance, she gave no sign of it. I wasn't even certain she saw us. It was like Hamish and I were now literally beneath her notice.

"Oh, I almost forgot," I said, taking my tote bag from where I'd left it on the neighboring seat. "I have some more happy eggs for you for tomorrow."

I handed Hamish the package Susan had prepared for him. His grin was enormous. "Och, Poppy, you're a true friend."

He lifted the brown packing paper from the box. Inside were two dozen eggs and a jar of honey. There was a note from Susan that simply read, *Good luck from us at the farm.*

Gerry swooped over to warn, "Now you've stepped in it." I looked up to see Florence walking the short distance to our table, laughter playing across her face. "I get *my* eggs straight from Susan Bentley."

Gerry struck an identical pose right behind her. "I get my eggs straight from Susan Bentley," he said in a falsetto. Then he dropped to his normal tone. "That woman is so annoying. I want to wipe that smug smile straight off her face." He pushed his palm around her nose and mouth, but of course, the only thing that happened was she took an instinctive step back. Gerry glared at me. "You could do it. Surely, you've got some magic trick that would work to make sure Hamish wins." I'd tell him later that, even though I agreed with him, I wasn't allowed to use magic that way. In the meantime, I tried to ignore Gerry.

I held it together, and so did Hamish, who was the one being baited by Florence. He said nothing, just shrugged and then made a great show of stacking up the two cartons of eggs and the jar of honey on the table. I watched Florence's expression change as she took note of Susan's generosity and the card the farmer had taken the time to write. *Ha. Eat that, Florence.*

"How was your intimate dinner at Broomewode Hall last night?" I couldn't resist asking. Maybe I couldn't use magic to remind her she wasn't quite as special as she seemed to think, but there was no law against sarcasm.

Florence flicked back her hair. "It was wonderful. We ate in the grand dining room. The countess had game pie served, buttery cabbage, lots of red wine, although I kept mine to a minimum to be fresh for today. The Champneys are such welcoming people." She shot me a sly glance. "They make me feel like one of the family."

I couldn't help but smile at the use of the word "they." I could have twisted the knife if I let slip that I knew Benedict hadn't been there, but right now I wanted to keep my burgeoning romance to myself. "That's nice," is all I said.

Hamish shot me a conspiratorial look and then handed me the menu. "What do you fancy?"

"I'm sorry I can't sit with you two," Florence said sweetly, "but I must get back to my producer. We have such plans." She was gone with a wave. Gerry wound up and kicked her in the backside. I choked back a laugh.

"It feels like my last supper," Hamish said, sounding a bit depressed.

"Nonsense," I replied. "Let's get you something hearty with lots of protein. You'll need stamina tomorrow."

He settled on a burger with Parmesan fries, and I decided I'd need lots of stamina to watch the final challenge, so I ordered a burger and fries too. What a good friend.

We talked through strategies that would help him stay calm and collected for tomorrow's showstopper. The last thing he needed was to get flustered. He was losing points on presentation, and mostly I thought that came from a shaky hand caused by nerves. Hamish was so accomplished. He was a police officer in Scotland, kept Shetland ponies, and baked like a dream. He was used to keeping cool in the most difficult situations. But now that he was so close to winning, he was letting the nerves in.

I couldn't give him magic, except the magic of friendship. I told him I believed in him and reminded him that most of Broomewode was also on his side.

"The countess is obviously in Camp Florence," he reminded me.

"But Susan Bentley's support comes with happy eggs and her special honey."

He laughed at that. "You're a true friend," he said again quietly but firmly. "I appreciate it."

When the burgers arrived, we ate hungrily. The meat was tender and full of charcoal flavor, relish, and mustard oozing from the sides. The fries were coated in a light dusting of finely shaved Parmesan—Ruta's handiwork at its best. We hardly shared a word as we wolfed down our meal. Hamish's quiet presence was a relief. He was tired from the pressure of the day and also full of longing to win, and I was exhausted and confused from finally meeting my mother, wondering who'd killed Charles Radlier, and also wondering what my future might hold with Benedict. Having my mother freak out about our relationship hurt. I barely knew her, and she disapproved of my choices. As for the countess, she couldn't have made her disapproval of me more clear. She practically snapped her fingers and called "Waitress!" when I was around.

Once our plates had been well and truly scraped clean, Hamish told me that he'd chatted with the Broomewode detectives this afternoon.

I leaned forward, eager for any new information. It was great that they treated Hamish as one of them.

"Obviously keep this to yourself, but the police are looking at Harrison Zucker as the prime suspect for both murders."

"Both?"

Hamish nodded. "They're convinced the two deaths are linked. And Zucker's affection for the countess did not go unnoticed—many villagers have commented on how he looked at her in public. If Zucker really wanted Lady Frome for himself, if passion had turned so dark that he was willing to do anything, why, knocking off her husband was surely the first step to winning her hand. And then with Charles Radlier stepping into the frame as another potential suitor, it would make sense to get rid of him as well. The man had means, motive and opportunity."

"You mean he's a serial killer?"

Hamish moved the eggs as though my rising voice might shatter them.

"They do say once a person kills, once they've crossed that line, it's much easier the second time."

Hmm. I still couldn't quite believe Evelyn Champney could inspire so much passion that a man would commit not one murder but two. I had to keep my personal feelings out of it.

"The only good thing about discovering a homicidal maniac in the local hunt club is that if Harrison Zucker killed the earl, then Katie Donegal is innocent," I said. Katie hadn't always been honest with me but I understood now that she'd been trying to protect me, too, in her way.

"I wasn't convinced Katie Donegal had killed the earl, but the evidence was compelling," Hamish reminded me.

"She claimed all along that someone had framed her. Guess she was right. Harrison Zucker was intimate with the family. Someone must have told him about Katie and the butcher having a feud via written notes," I said.

"I wonder how she's holding up. Must have been terrible for her not to attend the earl's funeral." Hamish said.

I was able to tell him that I'd visited with her today and she'd been grief-stricken. "She seems to care so genuinely for the Champneys that I couldn't imagine her doing anything to hurt them."

"But they were planning to fire her after all her years of faithful service. She had motive," Hamish reminded me.

I nodded. "And means and opportunity. I know."

"Unfortunately, she was also back in Broomewode when Charles Radlier was killed. And I've heard the key to the mausoleum was kept in the kitchen. She's not free yet, Poppy. You'd be well-advised not to see her alone again."

I blinked. "You think Katie Donegal would murder me?"

"Keep your voice down, lass. Seems to me odd things are always happening in Broomewode."

This gave me an opening to talk about yet another mysterious death. I decided that Hamish would be the best person to talk to about Mitty's astonishing revelation. I explained what he said about Stephen Champney's death—how convinced he'd been at the funeral that the viscount had been murdered either accidentally by the horse-spooking shots of the poachers or perhaps by Robert Champney himself. I asked his professional opinion: Could we really trust the memory of an old man plagued by the symptoms of his stroke? He was often incoherent, though there were definite moments of lucidity. Could it be that his memories of the past were fresher than the present?

"The earl might have been out riding that day, but that doesn't make him culpable," Hamish replied, having listened to the tale. "It's circumstantial evidence at best."

Hmm. It was exactly what I expected Hamish to say.

"Even if Mitty is right and Robert Champney *did* kill his cousin, he's already been punished. The man's dead himself. We couldn't charge him with the murder even if we had unshakable evidence."

And, twenty-five years later, what was the point?

$\mathcal{S}$ unday morning arrived with an explosion of color, the sun bursting up through the horizon in hues of orange and butter yellow. Unable to sleep, I watched the sun rise from my bedroom window at the inn, Gateau on my lap. Watching dawn reveal herself was a thing of beauty I'd only recently discovered rising for the early shifts at work. Once horrified by the six a.m. starts, I now found I enjoyed my early mornings. It felt like the birds were singing for me and Gateau, although given half the chance, she'd be out and about chasing them.

Still hazy with sleep, I tried to imagine how Hamish must be feeling this morning. I hoped he'd managed to get some sleep last night. So much stamina was required to piece each part of a (hopefully) jaw-dropping concept together. It went on that way for four hours, and with each minute, the strain and stress grew. The focus had to be unwavering, otherwise silly mistakes were made.

"Lucky it's not us, hey, Gateau," I said to my sweet familiar. "I'd thought I wanted to go all the way on the show at one time."

She meowed in a surprised tone.

"You're right. We do have enough on our plate."

I pulled myself away from the window and ran a bath. I had so many questions running amok in my mind that I hoped the water might be able to help me order them. If Elspeth was right and I was more in control of my visions than I'd thought, maybe soaking in the tub might bring some answers.

Lowering myself into the steamy water, I tried to relax. Although Valerie had promised to stay and answer all my questions, part of me was worried she might slip away again. There was something she was holding back, and I knew all the questions I wanted to ask of her would probe at a wound that still felt raw. Would Valerie finally speak openly? She held the key to my very beginnings, and it was only right that she should give it to me so I could unlock all that had long been buried and hidden from me.

I didn't want to be cruel, but I really wanted to know why she'd abandoned me. That sense of not being wanted had haunted me all my life. I'd felt the heartbreak of the young mother leaving that baby in a vision, but I'd yet to hear Valerie's story, and I knew my sense of my own history wouldn't be complete until she'd explained.

As I washed my hair, soft singing filled the air. I stopped mid-scrub and closed my eyes. There it was. No vision, but the same lilting, gentle song I'd heard weeks before and which Katie Donegal had confirmed was an old Irish melody. It was as familiar and comforting as the first time I'd heard it in a dream.

As clear to me as when Katie first hummed the song, unthinking. Now I realized it was my mom's beautiful voice singing me a lullaby Katie must have taught her. Was it a sign that I could trust Valerie wouldn't flee? I opened my eyes. My instinct said yes.

I took my time getting dressed, thankful that I'd managed not to spill anything on my pretty summer dress when I'd worn it to dinner with Benedict on Friday. As well as watching the final, the other past contestants and I were lined up to have a final on-camera interview. They'd interview us about our journey, our hot take on the showstopper bake, and predictions for who might be the winner. As if I'd reveal my true thoughts.

Banquet week meant this bake was going to be big enough to feed twenty people, according to the brief. I couldn't imagine having to do that amount of work on camera, knowing that millions of people at home were watching. But both bakers had done their homework. Hamish had pages of step-by-step notes that walked him through his complicated showstopper. He had to make six separate entremets cakes, arranged to look fit for a banquet. Like Hamish, I barely knew anything about this style of cake before the show.

AT THE TENT, a huge crowd was gathered, even bigger than the day before. This was the very last event. The Scottish and Italian flags were proudly waved, their cloth flapping in the gentle breeze. The excitement was tangible. I caught sight of Hamish and Florence setting up their workstations. Florence moved with confidence, practically sashaying around the scales and wooden bowls, as was her style. Like Hamish, she had a notebook next to her ingredients, but hers was closed. I figured Florence thought she had it in the bag. I closed my eyes and sent my well-wishes across the tent to Hamish, hoping that if I concentrated hard enough, my magic would take effect and transport some good vibes to my friend. I truly believed he could pull this thing off if he let go of the nerves and focused on doing his best.

"Hey there, stranger," a familiar voice said.

I turned, and to my delight there was Gaurav and his new girlfriend, Caitlin. He looked so relaxed in a black T-shirt and jeans.

We agreed that it was a relief to be out of the running.

"I'll miss seeing you at Broomewode," I told him.

He looked bashful and said, "I think you'll be seeing me." He kissed Caitlin's cheek, and she blushed prettily.

It was so nice to see Gaurav being sweet with a girl. He was normally so shy. Caitlin was clearly a good influence.

"Tell us, who do you think is going to win?" Caitlin asked.

I laughed and said my lips were sealed. "Have you seen any of the others?" I asked.

"I wonder how everyone is. It feels like a lifetime since I saw Priscilla and Daniel and Amara, of course. There were so many of us."

"And Gerry. Don't forget old Ger," my ghostly friend reminded me, pushing his way between me and Gaurav and putting his hands on his hips.

"Seems a shame Gerry won't be here," Gaurav said. "You remember, the man who was electrocuted the first weekend? What a tragedy that was."

Gerry twisted his whole body to stare at Gaurav. "He

remembers me. Somebody remembers me." He grabbed the young man's cheeks and gave him a ghostly kiss right on the lips.

To my amusement, Gaurav rubbed his mouth. "It will be nice to see everyone again. I passed Maggie and her children and grandchildren all piled into a white van on the motorway earlier."

"Looks like they're ready to start filming," Caitlin said as Fiona, the director, entered the tent, and the crowd was told to quieten down. The judges and comedians soon followed and, once everyone was miked up, Fiona called action.

I watched the scene unfold and smiled as Jilly stepped forward to introduce the day's task for the final time this series. She explained that the bakers were challenged to make six separate but complementary entremets for today's banquet theme.

"Entremets?" Arty repeated in a silly French accent. "Ooh la la, sounds fancy." He dropped the accent. "But what exactly is an entremets, dearest Jilly?" From what I'd glimpsed, with the two of them holding hands and kissing when they thought no one was looking, she really was his dearest Jilly.

She looked faux serious. "I'm glad you asked. These French creations have a long history. Originally, an entremets was a sweet offering, traditionally served up at banquets as a little treat between savory courses. More recently, they've become a way of chefs showing off their pastry prowess by creating a complex cake made up of various layers of different dessert techniques. Which also means this is the perfect pudding for the indecisive."

Arty asked, "So what should we be expecting from our bakers today? I'm guessing you're asking for the moon.

Maybe the stars too? How about the whole of the Milky Way?"

Jilly said, "In Old French, entremets translates literally as 'between courses.' *Entre* means 'between' and *mets* means 'course.' Because of this ambiguous title, the dish has had many guises over the years, with people adapting their approach to this old-fashioned favorite time and time again. The judges want to see our bakers do the same. By now, Florence and Hamish have both developed their own signature style. Elspeth and Jonathon want to see their adaptation of entremets."

She paused, and Arty continued, "But they also want to be surprised. The layers are commonly separated by a mousse, which helps give distinctive lines when the cake is cut into. The layers themselves usually include a light sponge, like a genoise, for the spongy texture. This slightly firmer layer gives the finished cake a sturdy structure so that when the center is revealed, it's beautifully streamlined. But the bakers can really run wild with the rest. We might expect to see set custards, pralines, and jellies. Imagination is the limit."

"Or your talent!" Jilly added.

Arty declared enough of the preamble, and just like that, the bakers had four hours to complete their showstoppers.

"We're not going to spend the whole time watching, are we?" Caitlin asked, already sounding bored.

Gaurav explained that we were going to be interviewed but could slip off for tea or coffee and a few sweet treats in the staff tent anytime. At that, Caitlin's eyes lit up. "Ooh, behind the scenes. Yes, please."

Gaurav put his arm around Caitlin. It was so nice to see

him this way. "Do you mind if we watch for a little while first?"

I looked around, wondering whether Benedict would come down for the final filming. I didn't see his tall figure among the crowd and felt a twinge of disappointment. I wanted to tell him about finding my birth mom, but that was one seriously long story, and I didn't know when we'd next be alone together. He had so much going on replanning his father's funeral and looking after his own mom, not to mention continuing to manage the estate.

I'd nearly been asleep last night when my phone had buzzed, and it was Benedict wishing me sweet dreams. I replied, saying the same, but then it took forever for me to actually fall asleep because I was too giddy. Who would have thought Benedict would have this effect on me?

My dreamy reverie faded as I realized Florence was already on the charm offensive with Jonathon, who was asking her to explain her showstopper design. My ears pricked up; I was intrigued to hear the design Florence had kept so close to her chest.

"Despite their complex appearance, entremets aren't as tricky to make as you might think. The key is getting everything perfectly layered, and that takes patience. So I've decided to stick to the flavor combinations I know best—those from my Italian heritage."

There was a flutter of excitement from the Italian flag-wielding fans. I tried hard not to roll my eyes.

"My six cakes all involve lemon from the Amalfi coast, but I'm playing with the texture differently in each cake and combining it with a complementary flavor. My beloved almond will be there, of course, but I'm also incorporating a tangy yuzu, some mango, and even papaya."

Jonathon nodded without comment. Was he at a loss as to what to say?

But Florence didn't need any prompts from Jonathon. She knew her lines. "I'm starting by making my genoise sponge, which we know already is a light Italian cake. I think it has the perfect kind of airy texture to make sure my entremets aren't too heavy."

Florence prepared the mix with ease, and Jonathon nodded approvingly as she talked her way effortlessly through her bake.

I watched, a little aghast, as she worked at triple speed. She lined three large shallow baking trays, scraping the mixture and spreading it across the surface, and before I knew it, she had already got her first bake in the oven. Now it was time to start on her jellies.

I turned my attention to Hamish. It was such a relief to see that he was also on target. I knew that Hamish's flavors were a little more traditional than Florence's, and each incorporated chocolate, berries and hazelnut. He was working on the mousse layer for his first entremets, a chocolate panna cotta and berry mousse cake with hazelnut ganache, which I thought sounded absolutely incredible.

Elspeth was questioning him on every move. But Hamish was keeping his cool. "My first step is to make a Swiss meringue. I'm combining egg and sugar in my mixer bowl, here, and once these two are incorporated, I'll take the bowl to the pan."

I watched, holding my breath even though Hamish was

doing fine, as he assembled a saucepan with an inch of water on low heat. He set the mixing bowl over the saucepan to create a double boiler and heated the mix while whisking until the sugar had dissolved. Even as he chatted to Elspeth, he didn't let his attention get distracted from his task. Hamish wasn't going to let any silly mistakes ruin his showstopper. Once the mix was finished, he transferred it to the electric mixer, and from there it would turn into a recognizable meringue whip, stiff but glossy.

Blackberries and raspberries were ready for the next stage. "How did we do that?" Gaurav asked me. I shook my head. My time in the tent seemed more like a dream now than something I'd actually done. On camera.

Gaurav was called away by one of the runners to film his "hot take" on who was going to win. I knew Gaurav well enough that he'd stay diplomatic to the end.

"It's very exciting when you watch the show at home," Caitlin whispered, "but without the TV edits, it does go on a bit."

I laughed. She was right. "Time flies when you're in the tent, though—doesn't matter how many hours you've got. It's never enough."

More people were arriving, and I was thrilled to see they included the past contestants. I excused myself and went to join them.

But any ideas I had of a happy reunion were quickly dissolved as we were all pulled in different directions and asked to give a final "on-camera."

The runner placed me in front of an old rose bush, its blooms heavy in the late June afternoon. While the crew set up the shot, I let my eyes travel over the vista before me. In the distance, the lead-lined windows of Broomewode Hall twinkled in the sunshine. It was funny how it was no longer imposing. It felt like home to me now. As did the grounds, the grandiose flowerbeds, meticulously groomed lawns, the ornamental lake. I had a deep connection to every part of the estate.

I smoothed down my hair as the sound guy miked me up. The same assistant producer who'd interviewed me on the week I left the show approached me with a smile. She said it was nice to see me again and that they were just looking for a quick sound bite where I reflected on my time on the show again and what I thought of today's bake.

"So, Poppy, if you could speak straight to me, not the camera, and tell us how life has been since you left the show."

I swallowed. I'd forgotten what it was like to be the center of attention. But with a warm smile from the interviewer, I explained that life had really changed since the show. I'd accepted a pastry chef position and was now working as a full-time baker. As I said the words, I accepted how different my life was from when the show had begun. I was still free-lancing as a designer, but baking had become my profession. I'd found my birth mom. I'd found Benedict. Not that I was about to share any of that with the film crew. I also had no intention of telling them who I thought was going to win. "It's a tight competition," I said, "with two such talented bakers." With Florence's talents a little more conniving than required.

The interviewer nodded and made a gesture for me to keep talking. If she was hoping for any dirt on the contestants, it was not going to come from me. I said, "Even though Florence definitely has the advantage at this point, I wouldn't discount Hamish. He's got a fantastic showstopper, and he looks like he's in control. It's still anyone's game."

"Did you imagine you would ever be on TV? How are you feeling about watching the show when it airs?"

I laughed nervously. "I mean, I'm terrified! I never thought in a million years I'd get onto the show, so I never thought about what life might be like once it's aired. The limelight is not really my thing."

The interviewer explained she was also asking each contestant to name their favorite moment on the show.

"That's an easy one for me. It has to be when I won best baker of the week for my cake rendition of St. Basil's Cathedral in Moscow for European Bakes week. That was a real highlight for me—the first moment where I thought I could hold my own in the competition. It really helped me to keep going." I grinned at the memory. There was nothing nicer than receiving a compliment from the great Elspeth Peach—and Jonathon, too, even though he was always less, well, precise with his praise.

The interviewer thanked me for my time, and then I was free to go.

Squinting against the sun, I saw the other contestants had gathered at the buffet tent and were happily catching up.

I joined them, letting myself be pulled into bear hugs left, right, and center. There was Daniel, the dentist, looking relaxed in a checked shirt and jeans, and Priscilla, in a multi-colored dress, with her trademark big hair and colorful glasses, telling him something that made him laugh. Ewan, the retired Welsh beekeeper, chatted to Amara, the doctor. They were helping themselves to cream cheese and cucumber sandwiches. Maggie and Evie, who was voted off right at the beginning, were deep in conversation about coffee cake. I felt a hand on my shoulder, and there was

Gaurav. "Isn't it so nice to see everyone again? It's like no time's passed."

I agreed. With the show in its last hours, it was truly the end of an era. There'd be no reason for everyone to gather in Broomewode Village again. I helped myself to a thinly sliced egg sandwich and joined in the conversation. It seemed like everyone's life had gone back to normal since their time on the show had ended. Daniel was back full-time at his dental practice; Priscilla was still cutting hair at her salon. Amara was rushed off her feet as usual at the GP clinic. Evie was back as an NHS administrator at her neighborhood hospital. The only person whose life had changed significantly was Maggie.

"Well, I couldn't believe it either," she was saying. "I mean, little old me being approached to write a cookbook. Apparently, they liked all the weird and wonderful baking hacks I've picked up during a lifetime of baking. Who'd have thought I'd have a new lease on life at my age?"

"It's perfect, Maggie," I said, squeezing her arm. "You're so knowledgeable about all kinds of baking. It's only fair to share that with the rest of the world. I'll be first in line to get a signed a copy."

Maggie laughed. "I've only just signed the contract, dear." But the twinkle in her eye showed her pleasure.

I poured myself a cup of steaming hot coffee and bit into my sandwich, happy to have a break from witnessing the intense pressure of the tent. It was good to be with the baking family again. But as I let myself relax, I couldn't help but wonder how this afternoon with Valerie was going to play out. It was exciting and nerve-racking in equal parts. All I could do was hope that she'd be honest and open with me. I was her daughter, after all.

Between visiting with my baking friends and watching the competition as much as I could stand to, the hours soon passed. The final scramble to get the entremets assembled with the minutes ticking down were finished, time was up, and the judging was about to begin.

"This is it," Gaurav said.

"Yup," I replied, "after all these weeks, they're finally going to crown a winner."

My stomach was as jumpy as though I were up there being judged. As difficult as the weeks had been, something amazing was ending.

CHAPTER 15

The excitement outside the tent had reached fever pitch. Flags were waving, and the crowd was gripping onto one another's arms as the judges came forward to taste the final showstoppers. I made my way to the front, squeezing in between two very zealous Florence fans. Oh well. I'd have to keep my face neutral no matter what the outcome. No one could ever know I was rooting for Hamish all the way.

But when I finally clapped eyes on the two finalists, I saw that they both looked utterly exhausted, propped up on stools at the front of the tent. All color had drained from their faces. I was surprised to see that I couldn't tell who looked more deflated, Hamish or Florence. Had the camera's darling finally run out of steam? She looked seriously worried.

And then I saw why.

All six of Florence's delicate and complicated entremets, which had looked perfect a minute ago, were beginning to deflate. It was like watching the air leak out of a tire. The layers were oozing. Was it the heat? Had she made a mistake in her ingredients? Not cooked them long enough? I couldn't believe it. And clearly, neither could Florence. None of her acting training could conceal the look of rage and confusion dancing across Florence's features.

My eyes scanned the tent for Gerry. I hadn't seen him all morning, which was suspicious enough as it was. But now there had been a baking disaster, and after his antics yesterday, I was sure Gerry was the culprit. Why hadn't he heeded my warning? Alive or dead, we had a responsibility not to let our emotions get the better of us when it came to messing with the living. Had he not listened to a single word I'd said? That naughty ghost!

Elspeth and Jonathon entered the tent. They were both professional enough not to react to Florence's disaster, but I could sense them both stiffening, a flutter of dismay in their eyes. Elspeth was the better of the two at remaining neutral. She smiled broadly and went to Hamish's bake first.

And what a bake it was! He had created six of the most perfect, darling little cakes I'd ever seen. Slim and elegant, multilayered and in an array of berry and chocolate colors, Hamish's showstopper was plated on a three-tiered silver dessert tower, two perfect cakes on each layer. It was beautiful. His decorations were the finest I'd ever seen him produce. I grinned as Elspeth complimented his presentation. "Well, Hamish, you have certainly saved your best work for the moment when it truly matters."

Hamish allowed himself a small smile and murmured his thanks. I could tell his heart was in his throat as Jonathon sliced into his first cake. It was raspberry glazed with elaborate white chocolate curls and fresh raspberries nestled in one corner.

There was a murmur of pleasure from both judges when they saw what was waiting for them inside, perfect layers of pink and white. Jonathon asked Hamish to explain the layers.

"You'll find vanilla genoise as the base, followed by white chocolate mousse, a raspberry curd, another layer of sponge, and then a mirror shine raspberry glaze on top."

There were the longed-for oohs and ahs from both judges as the forks disappeared into their mouths. My own taste-buds kicked into action, and I was jealous of the judges at that moment.

And the praise just kept on coming as they made their way around the dessert stand. Dark, bitter chocolate ganache met with sweet and creamy strawberry mousse and straw-berry sponge; blackberry coulis with a honey mousse in a blackcurrant dome. Each cake was topped with a unique flourish of edible flowers, fresh fruit, tempered chocolate, or chocolate fans and curls. Hamish had really outdone himself. I was bursting with pride. I wanted to shout, "That's my friend!" but managed to keep my cool.

What's more, the judges agreed. With each taste, their praise reached new heights. Even Jonathon, who was usually more reserved with his comments during judging, let rip with the good comments.

Modest Hamish was glowing. I'd never seen someone look so relieved. The same could not be said for his neighbor. Florence was visibly shrinking, just like her cakes. To Florence's credit, you could tell that they might have been fabulous if they had all risen properly. Her color combos were glorious: bright lemon yellow, deep yuzu matched with the soft almond and pistachio. It should have been wonderful. But something had gone wrong, and instead it was one hot mess.

Florence was visibly sweating. When the cameras trained on her, she remembered enough of her training to sit up straight and compose her features, but she couldn't hide what was happening on the inside.

"I suspect something went wrong with the raising agents," Elspeth said gently, not wanting to make Florence feel any worse.

It was pretty painful to watch as the judges sliced into the cakes. The layers had merged into one another so there were no clear lines—the very basic requirement of any entremets.

"The flavor is very good," Elspeth continued. "I really applaud your use of ingredients. There's your signature Italian ingredients but married perfectly with the Eastern influences of yuzu and matcha. It's the kind of sophisticated and complex combinations that we've enjoyed from you every week, Florence."

Even so, there was no getting away from the technical difficulties Florence had encountered. The judges announced they were retiring to the other tent to decide who would be crowned this year's winner of *The Great British Baking Contest*. There was an audible intake of breath from the crowd, and then Fiona, the director, yelled cut.

The other past contestants had gathered just behind me, and they huddled round, trying to figure out what had gone wrong for Florence. I didn't want to get involved in their chatter. I had a terrible poker face, and they'd be able to tell in a second that I was rooting for Hamish all the way. I was so happy he'd knocked it out of the park today. Yesterday hadn't been his day, but surely he'd more than made up for it with this spectacular showstopper?

I was about to head back to the catering marquee when a familiar bark sounded up.

"Sly!" Susan's voice scolded.

I laughed, shading my eyes against the sun to see where they were. Sly's ball appeared first, rolling towards me in a mess of grass and slobber. And there was the lovely collie himself, bounding over in a blur of black and white fur. He jumped at my legs, and I bent down to pay him some proper attention. No animals were supposed to be anywhere near the cameras, and Susan was likely in for a scolding of her own from the crew soon, so I got my cuddles in quick. Sly nuzzled into my hand happily. "I've missed you, boy," I said.

Susan asked me to fill her in. "Couldn't resist finding out the winner ahead of the rest of the world. Besides, I've a vested interest with all this use of my happy eggs. What have I missed?"

"I'm afraid your eggs haven't been able to save Florence from disaster today."

Susan didn't look surprised. In fact, she looked positively wry. "Maybe it's more a case of Florence not being able to save herself from herself."

"Susan, what are you saying?"

But my friend didn't reply. A small smile played around her lips. Surely she hadn't interfered in some way?

"Were the eggs...not so happy?"

"My hens can be prone to moods sometimes," she said. "Not every egg can be a happy one."

I couldn't resist a small smile of my own. Then we were silent. The judges were back to deliver their verdict. Hamish and Florence were brought outside the tent, and the crowd's eager chatter fell to silence.

Both Hamish and Florence were as white as Sly's snowiest patches. They were placed opposite the two judges and Jilly and Arty. For the first time ever, Florence looked frazzled. Her dress was still spectacular, but her makeup was slipping, there were black smudges beneath her eyes, and a few stray hairs fell from their place.

Hamish reached for Florence's hand. For a second, I thought she might refuse, which the cameras would catch, but at the last minute, she gripped his hand. It was nice to see them looking like friends again in this final act.

Jonathon cleared his throat, and then the cameras began to roll again.

"Bakers, we want to thank you both for bringing your warmth, good humor, and of course, your baking expertise to the tent this year. Elspeth and I had to make one of the most difficult decisions of our careers. Now I'm going to hand you over to my esteemed colleague, the great Elspeth Peach, who has the pleasure of announcing this year's winner."

Then I noticed that the smiles on Hamish's and Florence's faces were sincere. Even Florence's.

"She thinks she's got this in the bag," I whispered to Susan.

Susan shrugged. "And she might."

"It is with utmost pleasure that I can announce that the winner of this year's *Great British Baking Contest* is..." There was a dramatic pause. I inhaled deeply and held my breath.

"Hamish."

The crowd exploded, and happy cheers and applause for Hamish rang across the lawns.

He looked stunned. Lovely, modest Hamish.

"I can't believe my ears," he said. "Me?"

Jonathon grinned, his deep blue eyes twinkling with delight. "Not only have you been consistent, Hamish, you've really grown from week to week on this show, and by the final week, your presentation skills were nothing short of astounding. We're so happy to reward the focus and heart you've put into your baking—you're a real talent, and we've loved tasting everything you've baked."

Hamish still looked baffled. I desperately wanted to run on set and give him a great big hug, but decorum had to be upheld. No one wanted a past contestant to crash into the final scene. Florence was clearly aghast. She was trying to mask it but needed another few years of acting training yet. I could almost see the thoughts racing through her mind. How would this affect her TV deal? What would her new BFF, the countess, say? Where was her swanky producer friend?

Hamish turned to her, and the two final contestants hugged each other. Then they were all hugging. At a signal from Fiona, we former contestants were invited into the tent, and everyone was shaking hands and hugging. It was like a happy reunion, except for Florence, of course.

"I was so determined to be perfect that I didn't leave myself enough time for the baking," Florence muttered.

And there it was. Not Susan's moody eggs nor Gerry's antics had been to blame. In her determination to win at all costs, it was Florence who'd made the silly mistake.

CHAPTER 16

*B*ack at the inn, Hamish burst through the doors with a winner's strength and strode straight up to the bar. "Drinks are on me!" he declared. The rest of the bakers trickled in behind him.

"You might regret that," I warned Hamish. "There's no trusting this lot," I joked.

Eve was polishing glasses behind the bar. She caught my eye. "Don't worry, the series producers preordered six bottles of champagne for everyone. But we can let Hamish think otherwise for a little while yet."

I smiled back, but I knew my expression lacked enthusiasm. Eve sensed this—I mean it wouldn't take a witch to figure out that I might have lots of questions for my friend right now. "We'll talk later?" she suggested quietly. I nodded. Right now it was all about Hamish and his historic victory. I didn't want to start dredging up the past.

Eve passed Hamish and me a bottle each, and we cracked the gold foil, turning the cage until the cork was free to be loosened. Both bottles popped at the same time with a satisfying rush of air, and Eve handed everyone a champagne flute. Florence took two and headed over to the corner table where her producer friend sat. He didn't look thrilled.

As I topped up my friends' glasses, I caught sight of Florence in the corner having what looked like an extremely intense conversation with the producer. I didn't hear the conversation, but I saw him shake his head.

Florence was on the charm offensive, trying her hardest to smile, but I could smell her desperation. It looked like she was right. No one wanted a runner-up as TV presenter. Oh well. I couldn't help but think she'd brought this on herself. Florence had been overconfident. Drinking champagne like it was running out, dining out with the countess the night before filming, having business meetings with her producer when she should have been preparing for her final bake. If only she hadn't been so sure of herself, then maybe Florence could have pulled off a winning bake today.

The producer was slipping on an expensive-looking suit jacket, preparing to leave. Florence looked gutted.

I turned back to the other bakers and let myself be sucked into their happy bubble. With our glasses charged, we raised them to Hamish, and I cleared my throat, proposing a toast.

"I think we can all agree that a worthy baker won today. I'm so proud of you, Hamish, proud of how you kept your cool in the tent, how you kept pushing through the progressively more difficult tasks, how you handled each high and low with absolute grace. It's been a pleasure watching you go from strength to strength and even more of a pleasure to be able to call you my friend."

"Och, lassie, you're going to make a grown man cry," Hamish said, half-laughing, half-sniffing.

"To Hamish," Gaurav cried out, his delight bursting through his usual shyness.

The rest of the group echoed his words, and we drank from our flutes.

We settled around our old table, and it was just like old times again. Old times, except everything had changed. My phone buzzed, and a number I didn't recognize flashed on the screen.

I swiped the message open.

Hi Poppy, I'm at Eve's and Katie has gone to see Mitty. You're welcome over anytime. Vx

My heart leapt. My fear of having to chase Valerie down again had been for nothing. She was contacting *me*.

I wrote back quickly, explaining that I'd walk over shortly. I owed it to Hamish to stick around for a bit and give him a proper celebration. The rest of the show's crew began trickling into the inn, and before I knew it, there was a proper party going. Everyone was so thrilled for Hamish and relieved that another long stretch of filming had gone well.

Jonathon and Elspeth arrived last, fashionably late like the baking royalty they were, and I excused myself from the table to join them at the bar. I had my own special thanks to give to both judges before they left Broomewode. It was going to be so strange not having them around at the weekends.

"What an ending to an amazing series," Elspeth said.

"It's been a roller coaster," Jonathon agreed, running a hand through his dark hair. He looked exhausted.

"Has eating all that delicious cake taken it out of you, Jonathon?" I joked.

But Jonathon barely cracked a smile. "You've no idea," he said mysteriously.

"You brought it on yourself, my friend," Elspeth said, not unkindly.

"Guys, what's going on here?"

Elspeth looked at Jonathon.

"Let's just say I'm a little relieved the series has come to an end," he said. "It's been a bit of an ordeal for me."

Elspeth raised her eyebrows. Again, she managed to blend consternation with motherly concern. It was quite impressive. But I was still none the wiser. Was Jonathon ill? I suggested this, worried, but Jonathon insisted he was perfectly well.

He sighed and glanced around to make sure we weren't overhead. "I have a confession. I was appointed by the witches' council to be on the show this year. It wasn't my idea. It was punishment, meant to humiliate me."

"The witches' council?" I remembered Elspeth telling me about them once. At the time, I'd imagined them like the Greek gods on top of Mount Olympus, watching and sometimes intervening in the lives of the humans below when they deemed it necessary. But now that I knew more about the coven, I figured it was just a group of wise old witches who provided actual counsel for other witches who might need guidance either in their daily lives or for special spells. Maybe they wrote magic books, which I was yet to learn about? But I was straying from the point at hand.

Although Jonathon was a middle-aged man, he looked more like a sheepish boy than a baking celebrity right now. I turned to Elspeth, urging her to explain.

"Someone has been a naughty witch," Elspeth said, her tone still soft.

Jonathon's gaze fell to the floor, and he fiddled with the buttons on his blue shirt. He lowered his voice even further. "You see, Poppy, the truth is, I can't actually bake. I got through filming by the skin of my teeth."

"What?!" I spluttered. "You're Jonathon Pine. Everyone owns at least one of your five cookbooks. They're bestsellers! Your banana bread recipe is the best I've ever tasted."

"Magic," he whispered. "All magic."

He spoke so quietly, I thought I'd misheard.

"It started as a bit of a lark, but things got out of control. I became addicted to the fame."

I couldn't believe what I was hearing. "But you're not allowed to use magic for personal gain. It's like, rule numero uno for us witches. Even *I* know that, and I barely know anything yet."

Jonathon lowered himself onto a barstool. "I know, I know. Like I told Elspeth, it all started innocently enough. This woman I met said no man can bake a proper scone. Well, I decided to show her that wasn't true by baking her the best scone she'd ever tasted. All right, I used a spell, since I couldn't bake a scone or anything else, for that matter. But it was a matter of principle. And then one thing led to another."

What was it with people and their weird pride about scones? And it dawned on me. "That's why I found you rehearsing your lines in the rose garden that time. You had to plan what to say about each bake."

Jonathon nodded sadly. "Every week was so humiliating for me. I had to learn my lines so carefully. I couldn't afford a single slip-up. I've had to study all week long. I've worked harder than I've ever done in my life."

Wow. I was seriously shocked. "Well, you fooled me," I said. Though now that he mentioned it, I realized Jonathon was never quite as eloquent as Elspeth during the judging scenes, and he often waited to see what she had to say before offering his own judgment. Now I knew why. I chuckled. "Don't worry, Jonathon. We all feel like imposters when we're baking on the show anyway. I still can't quite believe that I've managed to make it my job. I keep expecting someone to pinch me awake."

"You're an excellent baker, Poppy," Jonathon said, "and you deserve your job. I don't deserve mine, which is why I'm going to announce to everyone today that I won't be returning next season."

"Is that really necessary?" Elspeth said, placing a friendly arm around Jonathon's shoulder. "You've been very popular. And you're learning every day."

"I've caught the baking bug, that's for sure. So I've decided to make true amends in the best way I could think of." Jonathon perked up suddenly. "I won't be returning next spring because I've enrolled in pastry school in France. Just call me Monsieur Pine from now on."

Elspeth looked as delighted as Jonathon. She told him that was a brilliant idea and applauded his change of heart.

"I never should have used magic for my own gain," he continued. "It was always going to backfire. It was too easy to become addicted to praise, and everything snowballed. This way, hopefully I'll get myself to a standard where I actually deserve the praise."

"Don't be too hard on yourself, Jonathon," Elspeth said.

"We all have our little foibles." She turned to me and explained that in earlier seasons of the show, she'd used a little magic to save some of the more amateur bakers from unnecessary blunders. "Catching a whisk before it slipped. Nothing too dramatic. I couldn't bear to let the little baking darlings flail and fail. It went against my nature." She hadn't thought anyone would notice, but of course, nothing escaped the steely eyes of the council. They saw each bend of the rules and marked it up against her.

"The witches' council were having none of it," Jonathon explained. Both judges had been handed warnings. Elspeth wasn't allowed to intervene anymore. There would be a huge price to pay if she did.

Panic shot me through me. Had I been one of those helpless lambs that Elspeth had rescued? I quickly asked if she'd stuck to her promise. Elspeth reassured me that she had.

"No tinkering, no magic to mention. I only wished every baker well in my heart—plain and simple kindness."

I asked what would have happened if Elspeth hadn't been able to help herself and ended up intervening. Surely it couldn't have been more serious than a slap on the wrist?

I was surprised by the answer.

"Banishment, for both of us," Jonathon said, his tone deadly serious.

"Banishment?" Whoa. I'd only just got my head around the coven and how it worked, and now I was hearing that membership wasn't a given.

"They can chuck you out? Just like that?"

Elspeth laughed kindly. "Don't be so alarmed. You have to really wrong the witch code of conduct for that to happen. But this is why you have to learn more about your witch-line,

Poppy. And now that filming is finished, I wanted to make a proposition."

I stood to attention, ignoring the growing noise of the other bakers' revelry behind us. Those guys were seriously into celebrating. Champagne corks popping and chatter and laughter meant at least no one could overhear my conversation with Elspeth and Jonathon.

Elspeth cleared her throat. "I would like to officially be your elder, to instruct you in the ways of the coven. If you're happy to accept, I propose one evening per week, and I will share my knowledge with you. I'll teach you everything you need to grow as a witch. You'll bloom and blossom in no time at all—as long as you put your mind to it."

Happy to accept? More like ecstatic! I nodded solemnly, my heart pounding with pride, and then began to grin ear to ear. I couldn't believe Elspeth wanted to help me.

"I don't have the words," I murmured. "Thank you. Thank you so much! It would really be an honor to have you as my teacher. I feel so much better about the future now."

Elspeth squeezed my hands. "While the weather stays warm, we can meet by the circle of stones. Just promise me no more gallivanting around, playing detective. I need you to stay safe."

I promised I would do everything in my power to stay safe and sound.

Elspeth let go of my hands and smiled broadly. "It feels like everything is coming together as it should. The best baker won. The young witch embarks on her education. The naughty witch is off to France to atone for his sins."

Jonathon laughed and excused himself to join the competition bakers, who were furiously waving him over. Now that the competition was finished, all fear of the judges seemed to have disappeared.

Now that we were alone, I felt like I could open up about everything that had happened in the last twenty-four hours. "I have news to share as well. I found Valerie, my birth mom. I'm meeting with her shortly to talk. I'm finally going to get some answers. I can't believe it." I caught Elspeth up on the seismic shock of realizing that Joanna was actually Valerie. How Katie Donegal and Eve had been letting her stay. How much was still left unsaid. I still didn't know the true identity of my birth dad.

Elspeth was delighted for me but had words of caution, too. "It's all coming together as it should. But stay on your guard, my dear Poppy. Whatever happened in the past must have been serious for Valerie to feel she had to flee Broomewode Village and leave you behind. Please take care."

I promised that I would, and when I checked the time, I realized I'd better make a move.

"Blessed be," she said as we hugged goodbye. "I'll see you tonight at the circle of standing stones."

"You will?" I was confused.

She shook her head at me. "Your first lesson. Keep an eye on the moon. It's full tonight. We'll have a magic circle."

I could hardly wait.

I joined the other bakers and realized this might be the last time we were all together.

I looked at everyone's happy faces. There was so much joy here. So many achievements and proud moments. None more so than for Hamish.

I lightly tapped him on the shoulder and told him that I had to go.

We hugged tightly. My heart was full. I pulled back and regarded Hamish's kind, handsome face. "I know I keep saying it, but I'm just so darned proud of you," I said, feeling a little tearful. "You're an honest man and a true friend. Promise that we'll stay in touch once you go back to Scotland for good? I'll come visit anytime."

"Of course," he said. "There's no getting rid of me now. We're baking friends for life ...that is, if you're not too grand for me," he said with wide grin. "I expect you'll be the next Countess of Frome before too long. Hope I'm not too humble to rate an invite to the wedding."

I blushed and stumbled over words and finally waved a general goodbye and left the inn.

CHAPTER 17

I arrived at Eve's flat full of emotions competing with each other. Excitement. Trepidation. Hope. Worry. Annoyance. Had all the secrecy around my origins really been necessary? Why did it feel like everyone was in on the secret about me but me? I felt betrayed, multiple times over. Mom or not, it was time for Valerie to give me more straight-up information and not so many mysterious hints. She'd downright lied to me when she posed as Joanna and said Valerie lived in Glasgow. Glasgow! The jig was up.

I pressed the buzzer, and Valerie's voice crackled through and told me to come up.

Okay, first good sign: no Katie. Valerie had been true to her word—we were going to be properly alone.

I climbed the stairs and tried to slow my breathing. Last time I'd seen Valerie, I'd been too shocked to think straight. Now I'd had time to think about what I wanted to say, what questions I wanted to ask.

Please don't let me down, Mom.

Valerie stood in the doorway. She was dressed in jeans

and a powder-blue shirt with frills at the neck and sleeves. Her long, dark hair was loose, her skin fresh and glowing.

"Katie's with Mitty," she said, gesturing for me to come in.

I was touched to see a spread laid out on the table by the sofa. A pot of black coffee, what looked to be lemon drizzle cake (a favorite), as well as a selection of chocolate biscuits. The afternoon light poured in through the sash windows, and I had to admit the whole scene looked cozy and inviting.

"I'm hoping to visit Mitty soon, too," Valerie continued. "I used to know him well."

A charge pulsed through me as Valerie came closer. "Coffee? Cake?" she asked, gesturing at the carefully laid table.

I nodded yes to both and let her serve me. When I bit into the sponge, I was pleasantly surprised at how delicious it was. "Mmm," I murmured.

"I baked it," Valerie said with a smile. "You got your love of baking from me."

Wow. Well, now I knew where my sweet tooth and favorable relationship with a cake mixer came from.

"He still remembers you," I said. "Mitty, that is. He called me Valerie only yesterday. It wasn't the first time."

Valerie curled up on one side of the couch and tucked in her feet. "Did he?"

"Yes. And he told an astonishing story." I sat beside her, and instead of all the questions that had been bubbling up in me all day, I found myself telling her the whole story of Mitty's insistence that the viscount had been murdered. As I talked, Valerie's kind eyes filled with sadness. I stopped midsentence. "Are you okay?" I asked, reaching across the couch and placing a hand on her shoulder. But as our bodies connected, I was suddenly filled with a sadness so overwhelming I drew back my hand.

"What happened?" I half-whispered.

Slow tears tracked down Valerie's face. "It's true. Everything Mitty said—it's all true." She swallowed and tucked her hair behind her ears. They were the same shape as mine. We were no longer touching, but the misery Valerie was experiencing flowed through me, too. I couldn't help it. My own eyes began to fill with tears. Mitty had been telling the truth the whole time. And no one had listened to him. I felt awful.

"So much pain," I said, touching the spot on my chest where my heart was beating terribly. "It feels like it's breaking, splitting in two."

"My heart did break," Valerie said, nodding. "Oh, it broke and it broke and it broke. I thought I'd never recover. But the thought of keeping you safe pulled me through."

I stayed perfectly still. I was on the cusp of discovering something so painful that the weight of it was almost unbearable.

Valerie wiped away her tears and let her gaze hold mine. "Poppy, the reason I had to give you up was because your life was in danger, too. Your life and my life—they were one and the same, because of your father."

I inhaled and held on to the breath.

"Who was my father?" I could barely get the words past the lump in my throat. I thought, finally, I knew.

"It was Stephen Champney, the viscount who was killed. He was your father."

I exhaled. The sound of my breath seemed to fill the room. I wasn't shocked or even surprised. On some level, I'd suspected this for a while even if I'd never had the exact thought. It was something that lived in me. It was more than instinct. It was something solid in my bones. I didn't have the words to explain how I was feeling, so I nodded at Valerie. At my mom.

So much was becoming horrifyingly clear. "Was it the earl, like Mitty thought?"

"Yes," Valerie said grimly, consternation replacing the sorrow that had been etched on her face just moments ago. "Robert Champney killed his cousin for his title, Poppy. That's why I had to run. He'd have killed us, too, if he'd found out about you." Her tears flowed again. "The only way I could protect you was to give you away. I knew the local baker and his family. The Philpotts were good, kind people. I knew they'd take good care of you."

"They couldn't keep me, though. I was adopted. By Americans."

She wiped her tears. "I was too young to understand that. I only knew I had to save your life. You were all I had left of him. Of our dreams of the future. Oh, Poppy, I'm so sorry."

"You did the best you could," I said, feeling again the pain and sorrow of that young mother giving away her child.

"You do understand what I'm saying?"

"Yes. My father was murdered by his cousin. You gave me up to save me."

"Poppy, why do you think Robert Champney would have murdered you and me without compunction?"

I hadn't liked the man, but I could only come up with one reason. "Because he was evil."

"I'm not sure he was. Greedy, jealous of his cousin, full of twisted ambition. He'd have killed you because you got in the way of what he wanted. You were the rightful heir to Broomewode Hall. The viscount's child. It was you and not his second cousin who should have succeeded him."

I was fuzzy about the laws of inheritance in England, but I said, "I was a girl and illegitimate, to boot. Was I really such a threat? No offense, but don't all British aristocrats have mistresses?"

Valerie shook her head. She looked shocked at my glib comment. "It wasn't like that. We were deeply in love."

My vision at the lake flashed back into my mind. It was of Valerie and the man I'd known was my dad, younger than they'd ever appeared to me before, holding hands, walking and laughing and so obviously in love, my heart had softened. But there was someone else there. Someone watching. Who was it? Was my bad feeling about the forest and the pine cones the sense that Robert Champney was there? Watching? Plotting murder?

But while I was on a terrible tangent, Valerie was fixed on a more pleasant past. A wistful look appeared in her warm, brown eyes. "When Stephen found out about you, he was so excited. We got married quietly in the village church. We didn't tell anyone. He wanted to be legally married before he told his parents, as he knew there'd be opposition. Even today, most of the old families wouldn't relish their son marrying a kitchen maid. Still, it was the happiest night of my life. The happiest night, that is, until you were born a few weeks later."

"You mean, you were pregnant with me and he still didn't tell his folks?" I was sure my dad was a great guy, but why not tell his family? Had he been ashamed?

She gazed into my eyes. "Your father wanted to please everyone. It was his nicest quality and his most aggravating.

He was going to tell his mother and father about us, but he wanted to be married first so there was no possibility of them stopping it. They were much more uptight than he was. Worried about what people would say. He didn't care about pomp and circumstance. His heart was big and pure. But he kept putting off telling them. Then he decided it was better to wait until you were born. Who can resist a baby?" Her voice wobbled again, but she cleared her throat and continued. "But he never had the chance. He was killed before he could tell his parents. Or anyone."

"I'm so sorry." My heart was breaking for my much younger mother, alone and pregnant, mourning her husband in secret.

"Everyone said it was an accident, but I had a vision. I knew it was Robert Champney. He was power-hungry. He wanted the title for himself. And I knew it wasn't going to take him long to figure out that I was pregnant and that you would stand in the way of his earldom. I fled. I gave you away to save your life. I couldn't let the two most precious things in the world be taken away from me by that wicked man."

Robert Champney killed my dad. I couldn't believe how many times I'd been in the same room as that man. It made me sick to my stomach.

"Most of the kitchen staff knew about us. Katie was a good friend to me. The blanket I wrapped you in when I left you with the Philpotts? That came from Katie. She risked her livelihood to help us—that shawl belonged to your grand-mother. Katie wanted you to have it to stay warm, but I think she also knew it would always connect you with Broome-wode. I believe she hoped you'd come back one day. Make things right. Katie is a wiser woman than you know."

So that's where the baby blanket came from. It was so satisfying to finally have an answer to the burning question that had brought me to Broomewode in the first place. But why hadn't Katie told me how I was really connected to Broomewode Hall weeks ago? I'd begged her to open up about the shawl and the painting. Yet she'd kept everything she knew to herself. "It did bring me here. I was watching the baking contest on TV one day and saw the countess giving a tour of Broomewode Hall. Behind her was a painting of a woman wearing my baby blanket. Only it was a shawl. I'd always kept that blanket, and I recognized it right away. That's what brought me here. Katie was right."

As if she read my mind, Valerie said, "It wasn't Katie's story to tell. The truth had to come from me. And remember, your life was still in danger. Even though you appeared to be an American with no connection to Broomewode, Robert Champney and his wife are very intelligent people. Cunning."

"His wife?" I knew I was interrupting, but the hairs stood up on the back of my neck. "You think the countess knew what Robert Champney had done? And said nothing?"

She gave a dry laugh. "I suspect Evelyn Champney modeled herself on Lady Macbeth. I'm not sure whether Robert Champney would have done what he did without the support of his loving wife."

I knew the countess to be cold and unfeeling. She definitely didn't want her precious son involved with someone who worked in the kitchen. Like me. Things hadn't changed that much in twenty-five years. But to think of her egging her husband on to kill his cousin made me feel genuinely ill.

Valerie continued, "When Eve discovered who I was, she

said she'd help me but only if I revealed everything to you. Don't be cross with her—she was trying to protect you. All your coven sisters are. You really are a lucky girl. Well-loved. So I hope you see why I reacted the way I did about Benedict yesterday. I could see history repeating itself again, and I was afraid."

As if she couldn't bear to speak another word, Valerie stood and went into the kitchen. She returned with a piece of paper and handed it to me. "This is our marriage certificate."

I looked at the innocuous piece of paper. "I believed you," I said. "You don't need to prove it."

Valerie laughed a little, a lovely sound that broke the tension of the moment. "I'm not trying to prove it to you, silly. The vicar who married us is still at the church. He'll support our claim." She looked very regal in that moment. I bet my mother would have been a much better countess than Evelyn Champney.

"I know you did exactly what you thought was right. There's no point thinking about the what-ifs. We have each other now, right?"

She smiled. I'd never seen anyone look so happy as she did as I spoke those simple words.

Gripping the paper in my hand, I told Valerie we were going straight to the church now to speak to the vicar. I wanted the advice of someone who'd lived here so long. Would he really tell the world he'd secretly married my mother and father? And what were the next steps? Lawyers and DNA tests? And then how did I go about the delicate business of telling the man I was falling in love with that I'd like his inheritance, please?

"Wait a minute. Are Benedict and I blood relations?" I

had a queasy feeling thinking this but my mother laughed. "I suppose so, but you're quite far removed on the family tree. Robert and Stephen were second cousins, so that makes you and Benedict, what? Third cousins? You share a great-great-grandfather, I believe. You don't need to worry about your children."

"Mom. We're not exactly thinking about kids." Yet. "I dread telling him. It seems like ever since I got here I've made Benedict's life more complicated."

"I'm sure he—"

The moment was interrupted as the door to the flat suddenly flung open. Surely Katie wasn't back already? I turned to face the hallway and got the shock of my life.

Evelyn Champney stood in the doorway. And she was wielding a shotgun.

"How did you get in?" Valerie demanded, moving her body in front of mine.

I reached for Valerie's hand and found that she was already holding hers out for me.

"We own this flat, of course. We own most of the property in the area." Lady Frome glared at my mother. "So, you are back. I thought as much."

"And this time I'm not leaving."

"Valerie." Lady Frome shook her head. "Valerie, Valerie, Valerie. You *really* should have stayed away. Was what happened to your lover not warning enough?" She laughed.

She sounded like a maniac.

The countess was dressed all in black, in drainpipe trousers and a fitted silk shirt. It was hardly the outfit of a killer. "Why don't you lower that rifle, Evelyn," I said as softly as I could manage. "You don't want anyone to get hurt."

"I'll be giving the instructions around here," she retorted sharply. "And I suggest you begin addressing me by title. I fought hard enough for it. Oh, the things I've had to sacrifice to get where I am now. You have no idea. None at all."

She edged closer to us.

"You can't shoot us in here with a shotgun," Valerie said, her voice remarkably serene. "It would make a horrific noise. Not to mention the mess on Eve's carpet, which you say you own. I know you're a woman of fine tastes. You wouldn't want to stain a quality rug."

The countess looked quite mad. "There won't be any noise. You're coming with me. We're going to take a little drive, straight to the cliffs. You can finally join your dear Stephen."

Anger like nothing I'd ever known flared up inside me. How dare she? I glanced at Valerie, and we shared a moment where it felt like our thought streams synced and then merged. We were two witches, stronger together than apart. Bound by blood as well as magic.

But the countess held a shotgun.

Could we really overcome her firearm with our combined powers? It was risky. We stayed rooted to the ground.

"Would you stop standing there like a couple of lost sheep?" She waved the shotgun at us. "Do come on. I've a great deal to do this evening. I've a funeral to plan. Again. Thanks to you." She glared at me.

And then I realized what had really happened. Katie Donegal hadn't killed the earl. Neither had Harrison Zucker. "It was *you*," I said. "You killed your husband."

"Of course, it was me. Do keep up. You're clearly not the detective you like to think you are. But I'm hoping there's one thing you do understand. All this?" She stopped speaking and swept her arm around the room. "All this is your fault, Poppy Wilkinson. If only you hadn't turned up in Broomewode Village, sticking your nose in where it wasn't wanted, snooping around, asking questions of the kitchen staff, it would have been better for everyone. And my dear husband might still be alive."

"What?" I cried out.

"Everything was fine until you came along. Everything was as it should be. We took our titles; we took our rightful place in society."

I swallowed. "You mean you know Robert Champney killed my father?" So Mom was right. I hadn't wanted to believe the countess had helped incite murder, but here she was pointing a firearm at us, which seemed like proof.

This time her laugh was more of a wicked howl. She threw her head back and let it all out. The terrible sound reverberated around the room. Luckily, she didn't hear the slight movement behind her. But I did.

My throat went dry. At first I thought the shock was causing me to hallucinate, but I blinked and saw quite clearly that Benedict was standing behind his mother in the hallway. Our gazes connected for a terrible moment. As much as I was worried for my own safety, I couldn't help feeling awful for what he must be going through. Valerie noticed him, too. I gripped her hand harder. We both focused on Evelyn Champney. I didn't know what Benedict planned to do, but I hoped, if he had to choose between his mother and me, he'd land on my side.

"Do you think Robert could have worked up the nerve to kill his cousin without me? Robert Champney was spineless.

When the tractor failed to finally get rid of you, he went soft on me. He thought we'd gone far enough already. He said maybe we could pay you off to disappear from here. After everything we had already sacrificed? No. Over my dead body...or his, as the situation played out." She chuckled at her own wit.

"Wait, are you saying what I think you're saying?" I was sorry Benedict had to hear this, but if his mother had killed his father, he had a right to know. "Did you kill your husband?"

I remembered her riding back from the hunt looking distraught, saying Robert Champney had fallen from his horse.

"Of course I did."

"And it was you who nearly killed us with that tractor? It wasn't an accident."

"If I'd operated the tractor, you'd be dead. It was Robert. Useless as always. He botched my perfect plan to get rid of two birds with one tractor. Simple, and the farmer would have been blamed."

"But—" Mom and I turned and shared a startled glance. "You know?" I didn't say any more in case she didn't know that the woman beside me was my mother.

"That you're Stephen Champney's brat? We've always known. Valerie was always going to disappear from Broome-wode and her spawn with her. However, we'd intended to take care of that ourselves." She glared at Valerie. "You got away before we could erase Stephen's mistake."

"Poppy was no mistake," my mother said, in true mom style.

Evelyn ignored her. "We'd come too far to stop. My

189

husband went soft. He wouldn't listen. I had to get rid of him. Charles Radlier must have seen something on the hunt that day. I had to move so quickly. I'd stretched the kitchen twine across the path earlier, making sure Katie would take the blame if it was ever discovered, but once the earl went down, I had to make certain he was dead, gather the twine and ride back to the hall without being seen. Charles either saw me or guessed. He thought I'd marry him to keep him quiet. I had other ideas. I prefer to choose my own husbands."

"So you lured that man into the crypt?"

"Yes. It was a brilliant plan. I said I wanted to make certain the crypt was tidy and ready to receive dear Robert. But I was frightened to go on my own. What could he say? Of course he came with me. I'd already pried the lid off an old coffin, knowing he'd bend down to take a look. I had a hammer at the ready. It was so simple. He fell into the coffin and all I had to do was put the lid back on and wipe the hammer. No one would ever have known."

I had never liked Evelyn Champney, but in my worst nightmares I hadn't imagined her as a murderer. Her eyes were cold when she stared at me. "Once again you ruined it. But you've interfered for the last time. My son is the earl, and no American kitchen maid is going to change that."

The shotgun was forgotten. I couldn't help glancing at Benedict. His handsome face had paled, but there was a look of determination etched across his forehead. His jaw was set. I couldn't imagine what he was feeling right now, hearing all of this.

A beat passed, then another. For the second time this weekend, it seemed like time had given up. My heart was in my mouth.

"Mother. How could you?" Benedict said, coming into the room. "You killed my father?" He sounded so shocked I wanted to comfort him. But there was his shotgun-toting mother in the way.

For the first time, she looked as though she weren't in control of the situation. "Why did you follow me?" she asked him.

"I was worried. I saw you go out with a shotgun. You've been acting so strange since Father died." He glanced at the shotgun and at her face. "Mother, please give me the gun. You don't want to do this."

He held out his hand, but she backed away, banging into the wall behind her. There was a terrible crash. She'd knocked into a circular mirror that fell from its hook on the wall and smashed. Great. Exactly what we needed right now, seven years of bad luck. If we lived that long.

"I've done it all for you, my beloved son. You must trust your mother. Now go on home and I'll be there soon." Evelyn Champney straightened and then raised the shotgun, aiming it at me.

Everything slowed down again. I felt Valerie gather her powers at the same time as Benedict threw himself in front of his mother. The scene revealed itself like a movie reel unspooling: Benedict's look of pain and determination, the countess cocking the rifle, fingers deftly moving to the trigger. "No," I screamed. Ben was sacrificing himself to save me. I put all my concentration on pushing the mouth of the shotgun up toward the ceiling.

And then time sped up again. The shotgun jerked towards the ceiling at the exact moment the countess fired it.

Benedict pushed his mother aside, and the shot went straight into the ceiling.

The sound was deafening. My ears rang.

And then just like in the café when the tractor was careening towards us, I felt Valerie's body cover mine. We tumbled to the floor. I was stunned, pinned beneath her weight.

I took deep breaths and then looked up. There were holes in the ceiling. Plaster was everywhere, and Valerie was coughing.

"Are you okay?" I asked, my ears still ringing. There was no response. I repeated the question louder, with more urgency.

Valerie nodded in between splutters. I looked around for Benedict. He'd crashed into an armchair. He wasn't moving. I raced over and leaned over his body. "Benedict? Benedict?"

"I'm okay," he croaked.

"No! Stop her! She's getting away!" Valerie cried.

I turned just in time to see the countess disappear through the doorway, her shotgun abandoned on the floor.

"I'll call the police," Valerie said as Benedict pulled me into his arms.

"I thought I'd lost you," he whispered into my hair. "My mother. I had no idea. I'm sorry."

"It wasn't your fault," I said, hugging him back. "You risked your life for me." We were both shaking.

CHAPTER 18

The full moon shone down on the circle of stones. I held hands with Valerie and Elspeth. We were beside the head stone, the one that loomed over the others, which were more weathered, some flat on the ground.

I still wanted to pinch myself to make sure I was alive. After Evelyn Champney left, the three of us had watched in horror as she'd sped off at a terrific speed in their Land Rover.

"How did you know?" I'd asked Benedict.

"I didn't. I saw Mother drive off with a shotgun, and I was worried about her. I had no idea."

Valerie told the police what vehicle the countess was driving and what direction she'd gone in, but Benedict said he was going after his mother "before she does any more damage. I'm the best person to find her. Perhaps she'll still trust me."

I thought of that woman so crazy she'd killed her own husband. "Please, stay safe." I took the protective amulet Eve had made me and whispered a spell of protection for Benedict. I kissed it and placed it on his wrist.

He pulled me into his arms and kissed me. Then he got into his car and went after his mother.

Valerie checked me all over for bumps and bruises. I brushed her away, half-laughing despite everything. She was such a *mom*.

Once I knew she was fine, too, Valerie reminded me there'd be a magic circle tonight for the full moon. And so here we were, Eve, Susan, Elspeth, and Valerie. My coven sisters and my birth mom. Despite having my life threatened yet again, I felt calm and full of love. The threads of my history were coming together, each loose tie finding its connection. I was grounded by my place in Broomewode history, grateful for the lineage Valerie had sacrificed herself to protect. It was sacred and special. My birth mom was special.

The sky was clear, and the moon smiled down on us. The air here was sweet and clean, and I took deep breaths, one after another after another, feeling myself revived with each lungful.

Eve and Susan arranged huge cream candles in a circle within the stones. I was expecting Elspeth to light the candles with her powers, but this time Elspeth stood back and turned to look at Valerie with affection. "My dear, why don't you do the honors?" she suggested.

Valerie beamed. "With pleasure." She made a circling motion with her outstretched finger, and each of the candles sprang to light, one after another, like a string of delicate fairy lights. Susan had brought sandalwood and oak moss incense and slipped a slender stick into a wooden holder. Valerie lit that, too, and a plume of sweet-smelling and earthy smoke entered the air. The atmosphere felt electric.

Susan brought out the crystals she'd used at other magic circles, but this time, instead of four crystals, each of a different hue, there were five. She kept the red for herself and then passed the green crystal to Eve, the translucent pearl-like one to Elspeth, and the two blue ones to me and Valerie. "Fire, air, earth, and two beautiful water witches," she said.

I couldn't believe I hadn't realized that Valerie was a water witch just like me. There was still so much to discover. But at least now I was on the right path.

We set the crystals down in front of us, the circle now complete.

"Sisters," Elspeth said, looking at each of us in turn, "we are gathered here today to welcome home our wandering sister Valerie and pay our respects to our lineage."

Valerie smiled. She was flushed with pleasure. "You have no idea how good it is to be home and to be reunited with my beautiful daughter."

There were murmurs of agreement from the others. I could feel the tears coming but tried my best to hold them back.

"Poppy," Elspeth said, "I think you should lead tonight's circle."

"Lead? I have no idea how!"

"Just take my hand," Valerie said softly. "It will come."

"Your mother is right," Susan said. "We all know the power has always been in you—now you must begin to learn how to connect with it."

I joined hands with Valerie and then Elspeth, and the

others followed until our bodies matched the shape of the stones and the candles flickering within.

A gentle ripple of electricity began in my fingertips, and then waves of fizzing energy weaved through my forearms and into my chest. It was powerful but not overwhelming, a force that helped me to connect with the coven and with the energy that coursed through Broomewode. I slowly closed my eyes. I remembered all the times I'd felt this nervous in the baking tent and a voice said, *You've got this, Pops.*

Gerry.

There was complete silence. No chirping of birds, no rustling of leaves. It was like we'd entered into a different sphere. Usually Elspeth would begin the circle with her ancient language of spells, but this time everyone was waiting on me. I didn't know what to say.

I expected to feel nervous, but instead I felt lifted up by the power of the circle, and before I knew what was really happening, words began to form themselves in my mouth, my tongue rolling over the complicated syllables. Quietly the chant emerged from me. The others followed suit, echoing the words I didn't know belonged to me, to us. This was magic I never expected.

The sound was enchanting: five women in perfect unison, in perfect synchronicity. Behind my closed lids, I was seeing colors. Rich earthy browns, rust reds, sandy taupe. All swirling together. Then blue appeared, deep and soulful greens. Each element was present. Earth, wind, water, fire. All of our colors combining and strengthening. We were syncing.

My body was trembling but not in fear—in awe of the power I could feel rising from the ground. Someone else was here.

"Dad," I breathed, breaking the chant and opening my eyes.

In the middle of our circle, there he was—outline flickering but clear to me. He was tall and slender in a pair of blue jeans and a white shirt with heavy brown boots. I realized now this was the casual attire he'd been wearing when he died, out riding along the cliff tops. But there was no sadness to his expression. His light brown hair was swept back, his skin tanned and smooth, and he was beaming at us. He turned to Valerie, who opened her eyes the second he turned to face her.

"My love," she cried. "You're here."

"I'm here," he replied. "I've always been here. I've watched over you both as far as I was able."

I felt their frustration that they couldn't fall into each other's arms. I tried to hold back my own emotion.

"You've no idea how I've missed you," Valerie said, the tears spilling over. "You're the love of my life."

"And you mine," he replied. "And our love lives on in our daughter."

He turned to me. It took everything I had not to burst into tears.

"I'm so proud of you, Poppy," he said. His tone was so earnest. He really meant it. "You have grit and determination, but most importantly, you have kindness, fairness, and love in your soul. You are the rightful successor to my position, and I know that you will watch over Broomewode Village and unite our community once more."

A lump came into my throat. "I promise I will always do my very best."

He nodded and then looked at Valerie again. "I love you.

Always." And with those words, his outline began flickering more strongly. I didn't want him to leave.

"WAAAIT!" A terrific yell crashed into the moment.

The women turned in unison, and then my eyes landed on Gerry. He was floating over to us at double speed, spiky red hair bobbing wildly, his car-and-truck-patterned shirt incongruous with the forest of beautiful trees behind him.

"Take me with you!" he cried. "Poppy's solved the mystery of her beginnings, right? Maybe that's what's been holding me here. I've been caught up in her search—but now that's over, maybe I can be over, as in all the way over to the other side?"

I laughed. I wasn't so sure Gerry was the ghostly detective he thought he was, but he *had* been a helpful sleuthing partner. With any luck, the countess was already under arrest and there would be no more terrible murders in the village.

My dad nodded and stretched out a hand, which Gerry grasped eagerly. It was a touching sight. Could Gerry finally get his happy ever after?

Gerry turned back to me. "Now that you're safe, I won't be your guardian ghost anymore, Pops. I'm gonna miss you."

"I'll miss you, too."

My father said, "You're going to be fine. But anytime you need me, look for the hawk. He'll be out there, sweeping through the skies."

A white light appeared behind him and Gerry.

"It's happening," Gerry said with awe. "Wooooow."

"Goodbye, my friend, and thank you," I said. "You'll be at peace now."

"Being on Team Poppy was the proudest moment of my life...well, my ghost-life."

Oh, Gerry, silly to the very end.

I turned back to my dad. So many emotions were rising up in me, but I took deep breaths and found that the simplest words were the right ones. "I love you," I said.

"I love you," he replied, and then turned to face the light.

Holding Gerry's hand, he led them forward, and the two ghosts melted away into the white light.

"Goodbye," I whispered. "I'll try to make you proud."

CHAPTER 19

*W*alking back down the hill toward the inn, I found I didn't have the words to express everything I was feeling. Eve and Valerie were strolling in companionable silence. Elspeth and Susan were discussing whether happy hens really influenced the quality of eggs. Everything was normal again, yet everything had changed.

It was bittersweet to discover my dad's true identity, only to have him disappear back to the spirit world. At least now I knew for sure where I came from and that he was proud of me. I would carry on the legacy that had been ripped from him by the countess and the earl. When we got back to the village, I'd speak with DI Hembly and Sergeant Lane to make sure they found the countess and held her accountable for her crimes. So many lives lost at her hands. And for what? A title? She really was as crazed as Lady Macbeth.

At least Gerry had made it to the other side. I was so happy he was no longer trapped in Broomewode. I was sure the poor haunted guests at the inn felt the same way, too.

Eve turned to me and said, "Katie's so happy. All the charges against her have been dropped."

"That's great." Though not surprising, after Evelyn Champney had boasted of killing her husband in front of me, my mother and Benedict. We'd all told the detectives what we'd heard. Poor Benedict. That must have been so difficult for him.

"She's really hoping to go back to work in Broomewode Hall," Eve said, looking at me hopefully.

"I'm sure Benedict will take her back. He's very fond of her."

"It's not likely to be his decision, though, luvvie. It'll be yours. You'll be mistress of Broomewode as soon as the lawyers get it all sorted."

I couldn't even think of that now. "Please, just tell her to go back to work. I'll talk to Benedict. We'll figure something out."

"Speaking of Benedict," Elspeth said, abandoning her chat with Susan, "I'd very much like to make your wedding cake. I've something special in mind."

I felt warmth and chills chase themselves up and down my spine. "Our wedding?" I felt breathless. "Elspeth? Did you have a vision?"

Four witches burst out laughing. Elspeth finally said, "I didn't need a vision, Poppy. There's a different kind of magic at work between you and Benedict."

Eve nodded. "It's true. I've known since I first saw the two of you together that you were soulmates."

"It's a practical match, too," Susan said. "It was Evelyn who had the wealth, you know. Which Benedict will inherit. While you'll inherit Broomewode."

I didn't care about any of that, except to be glad Benedict wouldn't lose everything he'd grown accustomed to.

"But they'll marry for love," Valerie said.

The path opened up, and I turned left to follow it back to the inn. To my right stood Broomewode Hall. There were lights on in the windows still. The golden stone glowed in the moonlight, giving no indication of the secrets kept behind its walls. No wonder it had always felt like home to me: It was where I'd been born. There was so much ahead of me, so much to sort out.

Lost in my thoughts, I almost didn't see the silhouette of a man emerge on the horizon. Oh, man! Had our spell not worked? Was Gerry back already? I raised a hand and squinted. It was definitely a man. A tall man. A handsome man.

Benedict walked toward me.

I waved back and then turned to where my coven sisters were trailing behind me. I motioned for them to hurry up. The four women picked up their pace, great goofy smiles on their faces.

"Head back to the inn without me; I'll catch you there in a bit," I said, trying to ignore their coy looks.

"Blessed be," they said in turn, as they passed. Eve with her playful eyes and long, gray braid; Susan with her happy eggs and happy can-do demeanor; elegant Elspeth, who'd been such an important witchy godmother to me. I was so grateful to have them in my life. The three of them linked arms like young girls and strode ahead.

Valerie hung back for a moment. She hugged me and whispered, "Follow your heart."

I nodded, solemn in the realization that my mom was giving me her blessing. I recalled how joyful she and my dad looked in my vision, the loving way they'd spoken to one another in the circle. Could I find the same kind of happiness?

I went to Benedict. His hands were in the pockets of his jeans, and his shoulders were ever so slightly hunched. He didn't pull me into his arms. He seemed distant.

"How did you find me?" I asked, smiling. "Are you a witch, too?"

Benedict laughed and took his hands out of his pockets. "No, but the moon is full, and I know what that means. It's been a long time since I was a boy spying on the coven."

He cleared his throat. "I have something to tell you. My mother has been found."

I exhaled. "I knew Hembly and Lane would come through."

He shook his head. "It was a motorway accident." He took a breath. "She was speeding and must have lost control. She drove the Land Rover straight into an oncoming lorry. She was killed instantly, but luckily, no one else was hurt. I suppose it's just as well. She'd have hated the trial, the humiliation."

I kept my thoughts to myself. She was dead, after all. "I'm sorry you lost your mother."

Benedict had lost both his parents in the space of a week. But they had committed unforgivable crimes. Still, no matter what his parents had done, they were still his parents. I knew the terrible pain of losing your family.

"I'm in shock, really. I went to see the vicar." He made a

face. "Another funeral to arrange." He ran a hand through his hair, smoothing it away from his eyes, which were full of an emotion I couldn't quite pinpoint. "He told me about your mother and father. He married them, Poppy. You're the rightful heir to Broomewode, not me. I'll help you. With my support, there should be no problem proving your inheritance."

"I'm so sorry. You didn't do anything wrong, and you've been raised to be the earl."

He cleared his throat again, and my heart melted a bit at how shy this great man was being. "I told you I wasn't meant to be the earl," he said. "I felt like a fraud. Now I know why. I was one. You're the rightful heir of Broomewode Hall. My family were usurpers."

"You're not responsible for what your parents did," I reminded him.

"I'll do whatever I can to help you take your rightful place at the house. Though I'll understand if you never want to see me again, Your Ladyship."

I gasped.

"You're the new Countess of Frome."

It sounded so strange to hear it out loud. But it felt good. It felt *right*. I was finally home.

I smiled and took Benedict's hands in mine. "Well, this Countess of Frome really wants a second date with a very cool guy she likes."

Benedict's eyes opened wider, and now I could see they were flooded with relief. He kissed me then, underneath the whitebeam tree, and for a moment I thought I saw a hawk swoop through the dusky sky, graceful and magnificent, watching over us with joy.

the oohs and ahhs of cooing admirers. Jeremy and I had been discussing would we or wouldn't we, but his fall put an end to that conversation.

Husbandless and childless, I no longer fit into their world. Honestly, I'd never really fit in. That part I didn't mind. It was Jeremy who had bound me to that group. Without him, I fell away like a badly-glued drawer handle.

When Jeremy died, did I think about leaving Willow Waters and going back to Maine? Of course, I did. But we had the village flower shop by then. Bewitching Blooms was my idea. I've always loved flowers and, when Jeremy was made redundant from his finance job in the City (that's London in Britspeak) and got a decent severance package, we decided to open a shop. He wanted a gift shop to fleece the constant stream of tourists who came to enjoy our picturesque village, thus filling it with traffic and tour buses and rendering it much less picturesque. I wanted a flower shop.

We compromised. Bewitching Blooms sold flowers and gift items. Our customers appreciated getting everything in one place, and we'd received lots of compliments. It made Jeremy and me extremely proud, which was worth more than making us rich. We could pay the bills, and that was enough for us.

Do we know each other well enough yet for me to tell you a secret? Let's suppose we do. But don't worry. This secret's nothing bad. It goes back to the language of flowers, a language documented even before Shakespeare's time. Rosemary for remembrance, pansies for thoughts, and all that. But plants do so much more than represent emotions. The right flowers, in the right combinations, are as powerful as any spell. Especially if they're gently helped along by an actual spell.

And so, when I did the arrangements for a wedding, I'd imbue the bride's bouquet and the groom's boutonniere with the kind of magic that gave them a propitious start to married life. When sending a bouquet to someone who was ill, I'd sometimes give a little strengthening boost to the blooms. A new baby? What new mother didn't need a little nurturing herself and a good night's sleep? For a funeral, I liked to offer comfort to the bereaved.

Naturally, I kept the added bonuses a secret, but people tended to order from me again and again. Not because they understood what I'd done, but because on a deeper, unconscious level, they recognized my flowers had helped them. The repeat customers were welcome, of course, but the real pleasure came from knowing that I was doing good in our village. What's the point of being a white witch if you can't share the love, right?

And so, on that auspicious bright Thursday in May, I opened my eyes, little realizing my life was about to change. No, that's not true. My cat, Blue, woke me. She's a pretty marmalade who appeared the day Jeremy died, confidently padding into my kitchen, where I was doubled over, weeping, while my thirty-seven-year-old husband lay dead in the local funeral home. I picked her up and buried my face in her fur. She let me, and I immediately knew she was destined to become my familiar.

We've been together ever since. I named her Blodeuwedd, who is the Welsh Goddess of Spring and Flowers. It's pronounced 'bluh DIE weth'—hence Blue for short, otherwise it's a bit of a mouthful when you're calling her for din-dins.

She was acting strange—restless, meowing, and headbutting me awake. Normally, it took several back rubs for me to even get her down to breakfast.

"What is it?" I asked, but she only glared balefully, as if I should know.

I blinked a few times, but all I saw was my bedroom. I still slept in the room I'd shared with Jeremy. Only these days, instead of his gentle snoring, I was lulled to sleep by Blue's soothing purring. My alarm was set for 7 a.m. to give me enough time to get ready for work, but it was only 6:30 and still a little misty outside. I groaned and tried to roll over, but I was awake now and somehow knew Blue wouldn't let me fall back to sleep.

Blue wasn't the most energetic of familiars. In fact, she was on the lazier end of the scale. Other familiars talked to their witches, strengthened their spells, did their bidding. If given the choice between helping with my magic or lazing around in the sun on her favorite spot on the couch, she'd go for the couch every time. After Jeremy died, she'd been a great comfort cat, and she'd clearly chosen me for a reason.

As far as I'd been able to see, her familiar talents came in two flavors. First, she was an excellent early warning system. Like now, when she was acting peculiar. That usually meant something unpleasant was about to happen. Her second talent was more nebulous. She strengthened my magic. If I cast a spell and made sure she was within my circle, it would be faster-acting and more efficacious. A bit like overdrive on a car. Pretty impressive for a little marmalade, right?

So the fact that she was acting so peculiar suggested that I should keep my wits about me. No doubt something was up and now that I was, too, I'd soon find out what it was.

Peony Dreadful is book one of a brand new series of paranormal cozy mysteries you won't want to miss. Sign up for my newsletter at NancyWarrenAuthor.com to hear about all of my new releases.

A Note from Nancy

Dear Reader,

Thank you for reading *The Great Witches Baking Show* series. I am so grateful for all the enthusiasm this series has received. If you enjoyed Poppy's adventures, you're sure to enjoy the *Village Flower Shop,* the *Vampire Knitting Club*, and the *Vampire Book Club* series.

I hope you'll consider leaving a review and please tell your friends who like cozy mysteries and culinary adventures.

Review *Whisk and Reward* on Amazon, Goodreads or BookBub. It makes such a difference.

Join my newsletter for a free prequel, *Tangles and Treasons*, the exciting tale of how the gorgeous Rafe Crosyer was turned into a vampire.

I hope to see you in my private Facebook Group. It's a lot of fun. www.facebook.com/groups/NancyWarrenKnitwits

Turn the page for Hamish's winning recipe for Chocolate Panna Cotta Berry Mousse Cakes with Hazelnut Ganache.

Until next time,
Happy Reading,
Nancy

RECIPE FOR CHOCOLATE PANNA COTTA BERRY MOUSSE CAKES WITH HAZELNUT GANACHE!

I couldn't leave you all without a final recipe—this time from my esteemed friend and fellow baking competitor, Hamish. I was over the moon when he won! And this recipe is a testament to his skill, patience, and love of all things cake.

It's the most difficult one yet—but don't worry, you don't have to make five other entremets as well! You're still a winner in my eyes. This particular flavor combination was by far my favorite of Hamish's six delectable cakes. There's just something so wholesome about berries and chocolate, and the hazelnut ganache finishes the whole lot off perfectly. The recipe for this bake looks complicated, but I promise it's worth it! Prep time should be only forty-five minutes with a bake time of thirty-five minutes. That's only an hour and twenty minutes—don't be put off by how many steps there are! The taste and texture are amazing: rich and creamy, cakey, crunchy, light and fluffy all in one bite.

Ingredients:

Chocolate Genoise:

- 3 large eggs
- 3 large egg yolks
- 1 teaspoon pure vanilla extract
- Pinch of salt
- ¾ cup sugar
- ½ cup cake flour
- ¼ cup dark cocoa powder

Simple Syrup:

- ½ cup water
- ½ cup sugar
- 1 to 2 tablespoons of Chambord liqueur (can be substituted with juice for those who like to keep it alcohol-free)

Chocolate Panna Cotta:

- ¾ cup heavy cream
- 1 teaspoon powdered gelatin
- 1 tablespoon water
- 2 tablespoons mascarpone cheese
- 1 tablespoon sugar
- Pinch of salt
- 2 ounces 70 percent dark chocolate

Toasted Hazelnut Ganache:

- ¾ cup hazelnuts skinned and lightly toasted

- ½ cup heavy cream
- 1 tablespoon unsalted butter
- 1 tablespoon granulated sugar
- 4 ounces 70 percent cocoa dark chocolate

Berry Mousse Layer:

- 2 teaspoons unflavored gelatin
- 4 tablespoons cold water
- 2 tablespoons lemon juice
- 1 cup fresh blackberries
- 1 cup fresh raspberries
- ½ cup granulated sugar
- 1 egg white
- ¾ cup heavy cream

Method:

Like Hamish, keep your cool and breathe. This looks more complicated than it is!

FOR THE CHOCOLATE GENOISE LAYERS:

1. First up, get your oven ready by making sure it has a rack in the middle and then preheat it to 400F. Line a 12x17 baking sheet with parchment paper— you might want some butter to help it stick.
2. Now for the good stuff. Whisk the eggs, extra egg yolks, vanilla, salt, and sugar together in a large bowl over a pan of simmering water. You want to be gentle with that whisk and make sure that the

mixture doesn't rise above a lukewarm temperature. Transfer the mixture to the bowl and whisk either with handheld beaters or your cake mixer on a medium-high speed until the mix has tripled in volume (phew). The mixture will be cool and thick, and if you want to test the texture, lift the whisk and see if a slow ribbon falls from the end back into the bowl. Got it? Good!

3. In another bowl, sift the flour and cocoa together and then add one-third of the dry mix to the bowl with the beaten egg. Now take a rubber spatula to carefully fold in the flour, making sure to scrape all the way to the bottom of the bowl to prevent the flour mixture from making lumps. Keep going with the process, working in thirds, until you have a smooth batter. Pour it into the prepared pan and then make sure that the top is smooth by working it over with a spatula.

4. This needs to go into the oven for approximately 10 to 12 minutes. Keep an eye on this! You don't want the cake to overcook and become too dry—if that happens, you won't be able to roll it properly later.

5. Once baked, let the cake cool on a rack. Once cool, carefully remove the cake from the baking sheet and invert it on a larger piece of parchment paper. Remove the parchment paper that was lining the baking sheet and then leave it be—we'll come back to him later once the panna cotta is set.

FOR THE SIMPLE SYRUP:

1. You can buy simple syrup, of course, but really it's not too much of a pain to make it at home. Find yourself a small saucepan and put it over a medium-high heat. Bring all the ingredients together until they simmer until the sugar dissolves completely, stirring occasionally. Once all combined, let it cool to room temperature.

FOR THE TOASTED HAZELNUT GANACHE LAYER:

1. This is my favorite part of the bake! Got any excess aggression? Toast your hazelnuts and then put them in a plastic bag and crush the lot with a rolling pin.

2. Now combine your cream, butter, and sugar in a small saucepan and bring to a gentle boil over medium heat, stirring occasionally. Make sure the heat is gentle—we don't want the cream to curdle. Once combined, take the pan off the heat and add in your chopped chocolate, using a rubber spatula to gently melt the chocolate with the hot cream. Now let it stand for another 3 minutes for the chocolate to fully melt. To blend the mix together, get a whisk and gently combine. Once it's cool, reach for those crushed hazelnuts and mix. Set aside.

FOR THE CHOCOLATE PANNA COTTA LAYER:

1. Mmmm, this stage makes me salivate. Take 2 tablespoons of cream and pour them into a small

heatproof bowl. Now sprinkle the gelatin (or veggie substitute) over it and let the whole lot stand until it has softened—this should take about 10 minutes. Once softened, make a bain marie by placing the smaller bowl in a larger one filled with hot water and stir until the gelatin has dissolved.

2. Now for the rest of the yum stuff. Put a saucepan over medium heat and bring the rest of the cream, the mascarpone, sugar, and salt to almost boiling point. When it just begins to bubble, remove from the heat and chocolate and whisk until smooth.

3. Combine the melted gelatin mixture with the chocolate mixture and stir until the whole lot is well blended. Get yourself a fine strainer, and then pour the mix into another bowl.

4. Now you've got your panna cotta mix! Cover the bowl with plastic wrap and slip it into the refrigerator until it has slightly thickened but not quite set. This should take about an hour or just under. Keep an eye on it—you don't want uneven layers.

FOR THE DOUBLE BERRY MOUSSE LAYER:

1. Almost there—don't lose heart! The first step for the mousse is to make a Swiss meringue. Do this by combining the egg white and 2 tablespoons of the sugar in a mixing bowl.

2. Time for another bain marie. Set a saucepan with 1 inch of water in it on low heat and set the bowl over the saucepan. Heat the egg white gently

while whisking until all the sugar has dissolved. It should feel hot to the touch.

3. Transfer the mixture to the bowl of an electric mixer fitted with a whisk attachment or keep in the same bowl and use hand whisks. Beat the mix on a medium-high speed until the egg white is stiff but still smooth and glossy. This should take about 8 minutes. Set the bowl aside.

4. In another small bowl (sorry about the washing up!), pour 1 tablespoon of water and 1 tablespoon of the lemon juice and sprinkle the gelatin over the lot. Let it stand until softened, which should be about 5 minutes.

5. In a blender, make a delicious-smelling puree of the blackberries and raspberries with the remaining 3 tablespoons of water and 1 tablespoon lemon juice.

6. You'll want to get rid of those pesky pips, so strain the berry puree into a small saucepan. You're aiming to make about 1½ cups of puree here, so if it's not enough, blend up some more berries. Now add the remaining sugar and bring the lot to a boil. Turn down the heat, and let it simmer until it's slightly reduced, stirring occasionally. This should take about 5 minutes.

7. Grab your gelatin bowl and stir in the reduced puree until it has completely dissolved. Let the mixture cool.

8. We're going to make a fabulous berry mirror glaze, so take about ¾ cup of the puree from this mix

and put it into another bowl with ¼ cup water. Set aside.

9. Now we put it all together! Beat the heavy cream until you have soft peaks, fold the Swiss meringue into the cooled berry puree, then fold in the soft whipped cream. Voilà. A beautiful berry mix!

NOW IT'S TIME TO ASSEMBLE!

1. Okay, team, you've done a great job getting each element made. Now it's time for the fun, creative part. You're going to line an 8-inch square pan (preferably 2 to 3 inches deep) with parchment, making sure the paper extends about 3 inches up the sides over the pan.
2. Cut out two 8-inch squares of genoise. Place one square of genoise on the bottom of the lined pan. Carefully brush with the simple syrup and freeze for 30 minutes.
3. After the half hour is up, remove the genoise from the freezer, and your panna cotta from the refrigerator, and spoon the panna cotta on top of the frozen genoise, smoothing it down with a spatula. Do make sure that the genoise really is frozen solid and the panna cotta is properly set before doing this, otherwise the genoise will absorb the panna cotta and the layers will merge.
4. Next layer is another square of genoise. Place it carefully on top of the panna cotta and press down evenly. Brush this with simple syrup, spoon the

hazelnut ganache on top and now freeze for about 45 minutes to an hour.

5. While this is going on, have a cup of tea, put your feet up, or you could decide to make the berry mousse at this stage. Your call. Either way, once the cake has had its time in the freezer, pour the berry mousse on top of the hazelnut ganache and freeze for another hour until the whole lot is frozen set.

6. Remember that reserved berry puree? It's time to warm it gently to loosen it. Remove the entremet from the freezer and pour over the top of the mousse. This is how you'll get that lovely berry mirror, which looks très professional in my opinion. Chill in the refrigerator until it has set.

7. Now for the final touches. Lift the cake from the pan using the parchment overhang. Carefully peel down the paper. Time to slice! You'll want to do this slowly, and we're aiming for ½-inch to 1-inch wide rectangles, depending on how many servings you need or how thin or thick you'd like them. As you slice, you should get some serious satisfaction from how beautiful each layer looks. Make each individual slice look even prettier by topping it with a little fresh berry or some chocolate curls or spirals, depending on how much steam you've got left!

I hope you feel just as much of a winner as Hamish.

Bon appétit!

The Great Witches Baking Show: Culinary Cozy Mystery

Gingerdead House - A Holiday Whodunnit

The Great Witches Baking Show Boxed Set: Books 1-3

Abigail Dixon: A 1920s Cozy Historical Mystery

In 1920s Paris everything is très chic, except murder.

Death of a Flapper - Book 1

Toni Diamond Mysteries

Toni is a successful saleswoman for Lady Bianca Cosmetics in this series of humorous cozy mysteries.

Frosted Shadow - Book 1

Ultimate Concealer - Book 2

Midnight Shimmer - Book 3

A Diamond Choker For Christmas - A Holiday Whodunnit

Toni Diamond Mysteries Boxed Set: Books 1-4

The Almost Wives Club

An enchanted wedding dress is a matchmaker in this series of romantic comedies where five runaway brides find out who the best men really are!

The Almost Wives Club: Kate - Book 1

Secondhand Bride - Book 2

Bridesmaid for Hire - Book 3

The Wedding Flight - Book 4

If the Dress Fits - Book 5

The Almost Wives Club Boxed Set: Books 1-5

Take a Chance series

Meet the Chance family, a cobbled together family of eleven kids who are all grown up and finding their ways in life and love.

Chance Encounter - Prequel

Kiss a Girl in the Rain - Book 1

Iris in Bloom - Book 2

Blueprint for a Kiss - Book 3

Every Rose - Book 4

Love to Go - Book 5

The Sheriff's Sweet Surrender - Book 6

The Daisy Game - Book 7

Take a Chance Boxed Set: Prequel and Books 1-3

For a complete list of books, check out Nancy's website at NancyWarrenAuthor.com

ABOUT THE AUTHOR

Nancy Warren is the USA Today Bestselling author of more than 100 novels. She's originally from Vancouver, Canada, though she tends to wander and has lived in England, Italy and California at various times. While living in Oxford she dreamed up The Vampire Knitting Club. Favorite moments include being the answer to a crossword puzzle clue in Canada's National Post newspaper, being featured on the front page of the New York Times when her book Speed Dating launched Harlequin's NASCAR series, and being nominated three times for Romance Writers of America's RITA award. She has an MA in Creative Writing from Bath Spa University. She's an avid hiker, loves chocolate and most of all, loves to hear from readers!

The best way to stay in touch is to sign up for Nancy's newsletter at NancyWarrenAuthor.com or www.facebook.com/groups/NancyWarrenKnitwits

To learn more about Nancy and her books
NancyWarrenAuthor.com

facebook.com/AuthorNancyWarren

twitter.com/nancywarren1

instagram.com/nancywarrenauthor

amazon.com/Nancy-Warren/e/B001H6NM5Q

goodreads.com/nancywarren

bookbub.com/authors/nancy-warren